*Index to Stories
in Thematic Anthologies
of Science Fiction*

A
Reference
Publication
in
Science
Fiction

Index to Stories in Thematic Anthologies of Science Fiction

Edited by

Marshall B. Tymn
Martin H. Greenberg
L. W. Currey
Joseph D. Olander

With an introduction by James Gunn

G.K. HALL & CO.

70 LINCOLN STREET, BOSTON, MASS.

Library of Congress Cataloging in Publication Data
Main entry under title:
Index to stories in thematic anthologies of science fiction.

    Includes indexes.
    1. Science fiction — Indexes.   I. Tymn, Marshall B.,
1937-
Z5917.S36I53   [PN3448.S45]   813'.0876'016
ISBN 0-8161-8027-X   78-14287

This publication is printed on permanent/durable acid-free paper
MANUFACTURED IN THE UNITED STATES OF AMERICA

Table of Contents

Table of Contents

Preface

This volume is an index to 181 thematic anthologies
of science fiction. It is designed as a reference work
for teachers constructing thematic units for sf classes,
as an aid to acquisitions librarians desiring to add
core titles to developing collections, and as a research
tool for scholars in the field.

The organization of the volume is by theme, or sub-
ject category. Under each theme the anthology titles
are listed in chronological order of publication. We
have cited the first published edition of each anthology,
but have not furnished complete publishing histories, as
this information is readily available to the concerned
researcher. Each title is numerically coded for easy
access; the code numbers are employed in the author and
title indexes. The title index contains anthology titles
and short story titles; we have not indexed non-fiction
contents of anthologies nor excerpts from novels. The
author index contains names of anthology editors and
story authors.

We would like to thank the staff of the Spaced-Out
Library, where the science fiction collection of the
Toronto Public Libraries is contained, for their help in
locating titles for this volume. We would also like to
thank Ms. Pat Puia for compiling and typing the author
and title indexes.

Marshall B. Tymn
Martin H. Greenberg
L. W. Currey
Joseph D. Olander

Introduction

From the middle of the nineteenth century, perhaps from 1818, what later was named science fiction existed as part of the general spectrum of literature, but the creation of the first science fiction magazine by Hugo Gernsback seemed like a signal to book publishers, critics, and libraries that science fiction was no longer the kind or quality of literary materials they need consider.

Science fiction was relegated to a kind of unliterary ghetto for a period of at least twenty years and aspects have persisted even longer. It was almost uniformly ignored by everyone outside the ghetto and loved, perhaps beyond reason, by those within it. Its amateurs, its lovers, its fans praised it, wrote about it, studied it, taught it, even prepared checklists and indexes of it. The love of the amateur recognizes no limits.

With a few exceptions, stories and novels published in the science fiction magazines were not reprinted in books between 1926 and 1946. Then the two major postwar anthologies, The Best of Science Fiction and Adventures in Time and Space, revealed the treasures buried in those crumbling pages. A wave of anthologization began that crested briefly in 1952, when Tony Boucher, co-editor of the Magazine of Fantasy and Science Fiction, commented, "It's doubtful if any specialized field can lay as much proportional stress on the anthology as science fiction does today."

Meanwhile, novels and some story collections were being reprinted by fan publishers, who got into the business with a few dollars, a friendly printer, and a plethora of enthusiasm and ingenuousness. Arkham House, founded in 1939, was the first to reprint H. P. Lovecraft and later expanded to include other authors. Many more fan presses got started after World War II, including Fantasy Press, Shasta, Gnome, and Avalon. They rescued E. E. Smith's space epics from the pulps, reprinted Jack Williamson, A. E. Van Vogt, Ray Bradbury, Isaac Asimov, and other fan favorites.

Then the traditional publishing houses became interested in the phenomenon. Simon and Schuster, Frederick Fell, Doubleday, and Dutton began to take over from the fan publishers and soon drove them out of business. Scribner's began publishing Robert Heinlein's juveniles, and Winston started a juvenile line as well. Paperback companies, particularly Ballantine Books and Ace, not only began to reprint hardcover books, but in the early Fifties they also got into paperback originals. The popularity of science fiction, if not its legitimacy, was established.

Books about science fiction represented a major breach in the ghetto wall. J. O. Bailey's <u>Pilgrims Through Space and Time</u> (1947) was a glimpse not so much into the ghetto as into the world before the ghetto. Kingsley Amis's <u>New Maps of Hell</u> (1960) was a major breakthrough, and the late Sixties and the Seventies brought the walls tumbling with a deluge of texts, studies, and histories, including my own <u>Alternate Worlds</u> (1975).

The process of breaking through the ivy-covered wall into the academy was even more difficult. The first regular class in science fiction was taught by Mark Hillegas at Colgate in 1962. The trend toward inclusion of popular literature courses of all kinds may have contributed to the acceptance of science fiction in the classroom, as courses began to spring up here and there, in high schools as well as in colleges. Science fiction, however, seems to have led the way for the detective story and the western, and courses in science fiction greatly outnumber other kinds of popular literature courses.

Everywhere the burden of initiating and carrying on the basic work of science fiction has been carried by the fan. The teachers of science fiction courses, even within the academy, have been science fiction fans, and Sam Moskowitz, whose life has been tied intimately to science fiction and its fans, not only organized the first evening courses in 1953 and 1954 for the City College of New York, but his research into the early authors of science fiction (published in Explorers of the Infinite, 1963, and Seekers of Tomorrow, 1966) and in late nineteenth and early twentieth century fiction and media (in Science Fiction by Gaslight, 1968, and Under the Moons of Mars, 1970) anticipated more traditional scholars by several years.

In the area of criticism, Damon Knight, James Blish, and others tried to bring serious standards to the field (collected in such volumes as Knight's In Search of Wonder, 1956, 1957, and Blish's The Issue at Hand, 1964, and More Issues at Hand, 1970) long before the people who make their living at it decided it was worth doing.

Although Thomas D. Clareson's Extrapolation dates to to 1959, the earliest semi-scholarly publications were published by fans. The most prominent examples are Leland Sapiro's Riverside Quarterly and Franklin and Ann Dietz's Luna Monthly. And it required Ed Woods's Advent Press to make a wide variety of critical books generally available.

Not only were the great magazine and book collections assembled by fans such as Sam Moskowitz and Forrest J. Ackerman, but the first indexes to the literature were compiled and published by fans. The irreplaceable Checklist of Fantastic Literature was edited by one fan, Everett F. Bleiler, with the assistance of many, and published originally by another, Melvin Korshak of Shasta

Publishers. The indispensable <u>Index to the Science Fiction Magazines 1926-1950</u> was compiled by Donald B. Day; and its successors, by the New England Science Fiction Association at MIT (the 1951-1965 index is attributed to Erwin S. Strauss). The first checklist of science fiction anthologies was produced in 1964 by Walter R. Cole. A similar volume, covering the 1950-1968 period, edited by Frederick Siemon and published by the American Library Association, was not available until 1971.

But amateur scholarship has its problems. Chief among them are limitations of time and resources; lesser but important are inaccuracy and incompleteness. As a consequence, the work of the fan, eagerly awaited, has been often delayed and sometimes poorly publicized and distributed. None of these problems have escaped the professional scholar, but the pervasiveness should be lessened.

The time is at hand, certainly, when science fiction scholarship should have the tools adequate to its needs. Scholars everywhere can greet with gratitude the first of what hopefully will be many new indexes to come, including a complete update to the Bleiler <u>Checklist</u>. One new reference tool is the recently published <u>Index to Science Fiction Anthologies and Collections</u> by William Contento. This index locates over 12,000 stories in over 1,900 anthologies and collections.

The compilers of <u>Index to Stories in Thematic Anthologies of Science Fiction</u> have designed a volume that meets a real need. For the first time in memory, teachers and scholars can locate a suitable story by its theme rather than trusting to uncertain memory, an exhausting search, or blind luck.

I have the personal hope, however, that the spirit of the amateur that has invigorated science fiction from its <u>Amazing</u> beginnings will continue to inspire the field now that the professionals are making their presence felt. The hope may be unnecessary: from what I know about the editors of this volume and of others already accomplished or in preparation, they are as much lovers of what they are doing as the most starry-eyed fan.

What you have in your hands is proof of that.

James Gunn
Lawrence, Kansas
February 1, 1978

Thematic Anthologies

Alien Encounter

1 <u>Contact</u>. Ed. Noel Keyes. New York: Paperback
   Library, 1963. 176pp. [paper].

   INTRODUCTION by Noel Keyes

   MAN THE DISCOVERER
   FIRST CONTACT by Murray Leinster
   INTELLIGENCE TEST by Harry Walton
   THE LARGE ANT by Howard Fast
   WHAT'S HE DOING IN THERE? by Fritz Leiber
   CHEMICAL PLANT by Ian Williamson
   LIMITING FACTOR by Clifford D. Simak
   THE FIRE BALLOONS by Ray Bradbury

   MAN THE DISCOVERED
   INVASION FROM MARS by Howard Koch
   THE GENTLE VULTURES by Isaac Asimov
   KNOCK by Fredrick Brown
   SPECIALIST by Robert Scheckley
   LOST MEMORY by Peter Phillips

2 <u>Earthmen and Strangers</u>: <u>Nine Stories of Science
   Fiction</u>. Ed. Robert Silverberg. New York:
   Duell, Sloan and Pearce, 1966. 240pp.

   INTRODUCTION by Robert Silverberg

   DEAR DEVIL by Eric Frank Russell
   THE BEST POLICY by Randall Garrett
   ALAREE by Robert Silverberg
   LIFE CYCLE by Poul Anderson
   THE GENTLE VULTURES by Isaac Asimov
   STRANGER STATION by Damon Knight

(Earthmen and Strangers)
  LOWER THAN ANGELS by Algis Budrys
  BLIND LIGHTNING by Harlan Ellison
  OUT OF THE SUN by Arthur C. Clarke

3 Encounters with Aliens: UFO's and Alien Beings
     in Science Fiction. Ed. George W. Earley.
     Los Angeles: Sherbourne Press, 1968. 244pp.

   EDITOR'S PREFACE by George W. Earley
   INTRODUCTION: THE FORTEANS AND THE FICTIONEERS
     by Ivan T. Sanderson

       Part I: Indirect (Nonpersonal) Contact
   THE FOUR-FACED VISITORS OF EZEKIEL by Arthur W.
     Orton
   THE CAVE OF HISTORY by Theodore Sturgeon
   THE UNINVITED GUEST by Christopher Anvil
   SOMETHING IN THE SKY by Lee Correy
   ALBATROSS by Mack Reynolds
   THE OTHER KIDS by Robert F. Young

       Part II: Direct (Personal) Contact
   THE GRANTHA SIGHTING by Avram Davidson
   THE TIE THAT BINDS by George Whitley
   THE VENUS PAPERS by Richard Wilson
   MINISTER WITHOUT PORTFOLIO by Mildred Clingerman
   FEAR IS A BUSINESS by Theodore Sturgeon
   RINGER by G. C. Edmondson

4 The Others. Ed. Terry Carr. Greenwich, CT:
     Fawcett Gold Medal, 1969. 192pp. [paper].

   ROOG by Philip K. Dick
   THE BLUE LENSES by Daphne Du Maurier
   SHIPSHAPE HOME by Richard Matheson
   EIGHT O'CLOCK IN THE MORNING by Ray Nelson
   THE SIX FINGERS OF TIME by R. A. Lafferty
   BE MY GUEST by Damon Knight
   THEY by Robert A. Heinlein

5   <u>First Contact</u>. Ed. Damon Knight. New York:
      Pinnacle Books, 1971. 219pp. [paper].

      INTRODUCTION by Damon Knight

      FIRST CONTACT by Murray Leinster
      DOOMSDAY DEFERRED by Will F. Jenkins
      THE HURKLE IS A HAPPY BEAST by Theodore Sturgeon
      NOT FINAL! by Isaac Asimov
      THE BLIND PILOT by Charles Henneberg
      THE SILLY SEASON by C. M. Kornbluth
      GOLDFISH BOWL by Richard [<u>sic</u>] A. Heinlein
      IN VALUE RECEIVED by H. B. Fyfe
      THE WAVERIES by Fredric Brown
      IN THE ABYSS by H. G. Wells

6   The Science Fiction Bestiary: <u>Nine Stories of</u>
      <u>Science Fiction</u>. Ed. Robert Silverberg.
      New York: Thomas Nelson, 1971. 256pp.

      INTRODUCTION by Robert Silverberg

      THE HURKLE IS A HAPPY BEAST by Theodore Sturgeon
      GRANDPA by James H. Schmitz
      THE BLUE GIRAFFE by L. Sprague de Camp
      THE PRESERVING MACHINE by Philip K. Dick
      A MARTIAN ODYSSEY by Stanley G. Weinbaum
      THE SHERIFF OF CANYON GULCH by Poul Anderson
        and Gordon R. Dickson
      DROP DEAD by Clifford D. Simak
      THE GNURRS COME FROM THE VOODVORK OUT by R.
        Bretnor
      COLLECTING TEAM by Robert Silverberg

7   <u>Bug-Eyed Monsters</u>: <u>Science Fiction Edited by</u>
      <u>Anthony Cheetham</u>. London: Sidgwick & Jackson,
      1972. 280pp.

      INTRODUCTION by Anthony Cheetham

      INVASION FROM MARS by Howard Koch
      NOT ONLY DEAD MEN by A. E. Van Vogt

(Bug-Eyed Monsters)
ARENA by Fredric Brown
SURFACE TENSION by James Blish
THE DESERTER by William Tenn
MOTHER by Philip Jose Farmer
STRANGER STATION by Damon Knight
GREENSLAVES by Frank Herbert
BALANCED ECOLOGY by James Schmitz
THE DANCE OF THE CHANGER & THREE by Terry Carr

8 The Alien Condition. Ed. Stephen Goldin.
New York: Ballantine Books, 1973. 206pp.
[paper].

INTRODUCTION by Stephen Goldin

LAMENT OF THE KEEKU BIRD by Kathleen Sky
WINGS by Vonda N. McIntyre
THE EMPIRE OF T'ANG LANG by Alan Dean Foster
A WAY OUT by Miriam Allen deFord
GEE, ISN'T HE THE CUTEST LITTLE THING? by Arthur
   Byron Cover
DEAF LISTENER by Rachel Cosgrove Payes
NOR IRON BARS A CAGE by C. F. Hensel and
   Stephen Goldin
ROUTINE PATROL ACTIVITY by Thomas Pickens
CALL FROM KERLYANA by William Carlson and
   Alice Laurance
THE SAFETY ENGINEER by S. Kye Boult
LOVE IS THE PLAN THE PLAN IS DEATH by James
   Tiptree, Jr.
THE LATEST FROM SIGMA CORVI by Edward Wellen

9 Creatures From Beyond: Nine Stories of Science
Fiction and Fantasy. Ed. Terry Carr. Nash-
ville: Thomas Nelson, 1975. 180pp.

INTRODUCTION by Terry Carr

THE WORM by David H. Keller
MIMIC by Donald A. Wollheim

<u>(Creatures From Beyond)</u>
  IT by Theodore Sturgeon
  BEAUTY AND THE BEAST by Henry Kuttner
  SOME ARE BORN CATS by Terry and Carol Carr
  FULL SUN by Brian W. Aldiss
  THE SILENT COLONY by Robert Silverberg
  THE STREET THAT WASN'T THERE by Clifford D.
    Simak and Carl Jacobi
  DEAR DEVIL by Eric Frank Russell

10   <u>The Aliens</u>: <u>Seven Stories of Science Fiction</u>.
     Ed. Robert Silverberg. Nashville: Thomas
     Nelson, 1976. 189pp.

     INTRODUCTION by Robert Silverberg

     AN EYE FOR A WHAT? by Damon Knight
     HOP-FRIEND by Terry Carr
     FIREWATER by William Tenn
     ARENA by Fredric Brown
     COUNTERCHARM by James White
     LOOK, YOU THINK YOU'VE GOT TROUBLES by Carol
       Carr
     SUNDANCE by Robert Silverberg

Alternate Worlds

(If It Had Happened Otherwise)
    IF NAPOLEON HAD WON THE BATTLE OF WATERLOO by
        Sir George Trevelyan
    IF ARCHDUKE FERDINAND HAD NOT LOVED HIS WIFE by
        A. J. P. Taylor

12   Worlds of Maybe: Seven Stories of Science Fic-
        tion. Ed. Robert Silverberg. New York:
        Thomas Nelson, 1970. 256pp.

    INTRODUCTION by Robert Silverberg

    SIDEWISE IN TIME by Murray Leinster
    SAIL ON! SAIL ON! by Philip José Farmer
    SLIPS TAKE OVER by Miriam Allen deFord
    ALL THE MYRIAD WAYS by Larry Niven
    LIVING SPACE by Isaac Asimov
    TRANSLATION ERROR by Robert Silverberg
    DELENDA EST by Poul Anderson

13   Beyond Time. Ed. Sandra Ley. New York: Pocket
        Books, 1976. 268pp. [paper].

    INTRODUCTION by Sandra Ley

    THE CLIOMETRICON by George Zebrowski
    THE RISING OF THE SUN by Gordon Eklund
    JUPITER LAUGHS by Edmund Cooper
    WORLDS ENOUGH by Don Thompson
    ASSAULT ON FAT MOUNTAIN by R. A. Lafferty
    O BRAVE NEW WORLD! by Avram Davidson
    HAIL TO THE CHIEF by Lucy Cores
    SOY LA LIBERTAD by Robert Coulson
    THE DEVIL AND THE DEEP BLUE SKY by Robert
        Chilson
    A CLASS WITH DR. CHANG by Ward Moore
    UNSCHEDULED FLIGHT by Juanita Coulson
    ALTERNATE UNIVERSE I, II, III by Tom Disch
    POLONAISE by Alan Dean Foster
    U-GENIE SX-1-HUMAN ENTREPRENEUR: NATURALLY
        RAPACIOUS YANKEE by Dimitri V. Gat

Animals

14 Satan's Pets. Ed. Vic Ghidalia. New York:
Manor Books, 1972. 224pp. [paper].

OUT IN THE GARDEN by Philip K. Dick
LEGACY OF TERROR by Henry Slesar
THE DOGS OF DOCTOR DWANN by Edmond Hamilton
LEFTY FEEP GETS HENPECKED by Robert Bloch
THE RAT RACKET by David H. Keller, M.D.
KEYHOLE by Murray Leinster
THANKS FROM THE WHOLE BOUQUET by Harvey Jacobs
THE REMARKABLE TALENT OF EGBERT HAW by Nelson
    Bond
THE ANIMALS IN THE CASE by H. Russell Wakefield
THE CAT by E. F. Benson

15 Zoo 2000: Twelve Stories of Science Fiction and
Fantasy Beasts. Comp. Jane Yolen. New York:
Seabury Press, 1973. 224pp.

INTRODUCTION by Jane Yolen

ZOO 2000 by Richard Curtis
THE HURKLE IS A HAPPY BEAST by Theodore Sturgeon
THE DEEP RANGE by Arthur C. Clarke
THERE IS A WOLF IN MY TIME MACHINE by Larry
    Niven
APPLE by John Baxter
INTERVIEW WITH A LEMMING by James Thurber
ALL CATS ARE GREY by Andre Norton
THE MOUSE by Howard Fast
THE ISLAND OF THE ENDANGERED by Dale Ferguson
COUNTRY DOCTOR by William Morrison

Animals

Anthropology

16 Apeman, Spaceman: Anthropological Science Fiction. Ed. Leon E. Stover and Harry Harrison.
   New York: Doubleday, 1968. 355pp.

FOREWORD by Carleton S. Coon
INTRODUCTION by Leon E. Stover and Harry
  Harrison

MAN...

    FOSSILS
NEANDERTHAL by Marijane Allen [poem]
THROWBACK by L. Sprague de Camp

    THE HAIRLESS APE
APOLOGY FOR MAN'S PHYSIQUE by Earnest A. Hooton
  [essay]
THE RENEGADE by Lester del Rey

    DOMINANT SPECIES
ELTONIAN PYRAMID by Ralph W. Dexter [essay]
GOLDFISH BOWL by Robert A. Heinlein
THE SECOND-CLASS CITIZEN by Damon Knight
CULTURE by Jerry Shelton

    UNFINISHED EVOLUTION
THE MAN OF THE YEAR MILLION by H. G. Wells
1,000,000 A.D. [anonymous] [poem]
THE FUTURE OF THE RACES OF MAN by Carleton S.
  Coon [essay]

...AND HIS WORKS

    PREHISTORY
THE EVOLUTION MAN by Roy Lewis

13

(Apeman, Spaceman)
THE KON-TIKI MYTH by Robert C. Suggs [essay]
A MEDAL FOR HORATIUS by Brig. Gen. William C.
  Hall

  ARCHAEOLOGY
OMNILINGUAL by H. Beam Piper
FOR THOSE WHO FOLLOW AFTER by Dean McLaughlin
A PRELIMINARY INVESTIGATION OF AN EARLY MAN
  SITE IN THE DELAWARE RIVER VALLEY by Charles
  W. Ward and Timothy J. O'Leary

  LOCAL CUSTOMS
BODY RITUAL AMONG THE NACIREMA by Horace M.
  Miner
THE WAIT by Kit Reed
EVERBODYOVSKYISM IN CAT CITY by Lao Shaw
  [excerpt]
THE NINE BILLION NAMES OF GOD by Arthur C.
  Clarke
PEANUTS by Charles M. Schulz [cartoon]

  APPLIED ANTHROPOLOGY
THE CAPTIVES by Julian Chain
MEN IN SPACE by Harold D. Lasswell [essay]
OF COURSE by Chad Oliver

AFTERWORD by Leon E. Stover

REFERENCES CITED

17 Anthropology Through Science Fiction. Ed. Carol
    Mason, Martin Harry Greenberg and Patricia
    Warrick. New York: St. Martin's Press, 1974.
    387pp.

    INTRODUCTION by the Editors

      1: MAN AS PART OF NATURE
    A MARTIAN ODYSSEY by Stanley G. Weinbaum
    ARENA by Fredric Brown

Anthropology

Artificial Life Forms

18   <u>The Robot and the Man</u>. Ed. Martin Greenberg.
     New York: Gnome Press, 1953. 251pp.

     THE MECHANICAL ANSWER by John D. MacDonald
     SELF PORTRAIT by Bernard Wolfe
     DEADLOCK by Lewis Padgett
     ROBINIC by H. H. Holmes
     BURNING BRIGHT by John S. Browning
     FINAL COMMAND by A. E. Van Vogt
     THOUGH DREAMERS DIE by Lester del Rey
     RUST by Joseph E. Kelleam
     ROBOTS RETURN by Robert Moore Williams
     INTO THY HANDS by Lester del Rey

19   <u>Science Fiction Thinking Machines: Robots,
     Androids, Computers</u>. Ed. Groff Conklin.
     New York: Vanguard Press, 1954. 367pp.

     INTRODUCTION by Groff Conklin

        PART ONE: ROBOTS
     AUTOMATA: I by S. Fowler Wright
     MOXON'S MASTER by Ambrose Bierce
     ROBBIE by Isaac Asimov
     THE SCARAB by Raymond Z. Gallun
     THE MECHANICAL BRIDE by Fritz Leiber
     VIRTUOSO by Herbert Goldstone
     AUTOMATA: II by S. Fowler Wright
     BOOMERANG by Eric Frank Russell
     THE JESTER by William Tenn
     R.U.R. by Karel Capek [play]
     SKIRMISH by Clifford D. Simak

(Science Fiction Thinking Machines)
SOLDIER BOY by Michael Shaara
AUTOMATA: III by S. Fowler Wright
MEN ARE DIFFERENT by Alan Bloch

PART TWO: ANDROIDS
LETTER TO ELLEN by Chan Davis
SCULPTORS OF LIFE by Wallace West
THE GOLDEN EGG by Theodore Sturgeon
DEAD END by Wallace MacFarlane

PART THREE: COMPUTERS
ANSWER by Hal Clement
SAM HALL by Poul Anderson
DUMB WAITER by Walter M. Miller, Jr.
PROBLEM FOR EMMY by Robert Sherman Townes

SELECTED LIST OF TALES ABOUT ROBOTS, ANDROIDS,
   AND COMPUTERS

20   The Coming of the Robots. Ed. Sam Moskowitz.
      New York: Collier Books, 1963. 254pp. [paper].

      I, ROBOT by Eando Binder
      HELEN O'LOY by Lester del Rey
      THE LOST MACHINE by John Wyndham
      RUNAROUND by Isaac Asimov
      EARTH FOR INSPIRATION by Clifford D. Simak
      LOST MEMORY by Peter Phillips
      REX by Harl Vincent
      TRUE CONFESSION by F. Orlin Tremaine
      DERELICT by Raymond Z. Gallun
      MISFIT by Michael Fischer

21   Invasion of the Robots. Ed. Roger Elwood.
      New York: Paperback Library, 1965. 157pp.
      [paper].

      INTRODUCTION by Roger Elwood

      SATISFACTION GUARANTEED by Isaac Asimov
      PIGGY BANK by Henry Kuttner

(Invasion of the Robots)
WITH FOLDED HANDS by Jack Williamson
BROTHER TO THE MACHINE by Richard Matheson
THE DEFENDERS by Philip K. Dick
ALMOST HUMAN by Robert Bloch
INTO THY HANDS by Lester del Rey
BOOMERANG by Eric Frank Russell

22   The Pseudo-People: Androids in Science Fiction.
     Ed. William F. Nolan. Los Angeles: Sherbourne
     Press, 1965. 238pp.

     EDITOR'S PREFACE: A IS FOR ANDROID by William
       F. Nolan
     INTRODUCTION by A. E. Van Vogt

     THOSE AMONG US by Henry Kuttner
     CHANGELING by Ray Bradbury
     THE ADDICT by Shelly Lowenkopf
     THE LIFE GAME by Chad Oliver
     EVIDENCE by Isaac Asimov
     THE SHOW MUST GO ON by James Causey
     GEEVER'S FLIGHT by Charles E. Fritch
     THE FIRES OF NIGHT by Dennis Etchison
     STEEL by Richard Matheson
     BADINAGE by Ron Goulart
     JUKE DOLL by Robert F. Young
     LAST RITES by Charles Beaumont
     THE FASTERFASTER AFFAIR by Frank Anmar
     THE JOY OF LIVING by William F. Nolan

     A BIBLIOGRAPHY OF ROBOT FICTION

23   The Metal Smile. Ed. Damon Knight. New York:
     Belmont Books, 1968. 158pp. [paper].

     THE NEW FATHER CHRISTMAS by Brian W. Aldiss
     ANSWER by Fredric Brown
     FOOL'S MATE by Robert Sheckley
     QUIXOTE AND THE WINDMILL by Poul Anderson
     TWO-HANDED ENGINE by Henry Kuttner and C. L.
       Moore

(The Metal Smile)
    FIRST TO SERVE by Algis Budrys
    I MADE YOU by Walter M. Miller
    MONKEY WRENCH by Gordon R. Dickson
    IMPOSTER by Philip K. Dick
    SOMEDAY by Isaac Asimov
    SHORT IN THE CHEST by Idris Seabright
    NIGHTMARE NUMBER THREE by Stephen Vincent Benét

24   Human-Machines: An Anthology of Stories About
        Cyborgs. Ed. by Thomas N. Scortia and George
        Zebrowski. New York: Vintage Books, 1975.
        252pp. [paper].

     INTRODUCTION: "UNHOLY MARRIAGE": THE CYBORG
        IN SCIENCE FICTION by Thomas N. Scortia and
        George Zebrowski

     MEN OF IRON by Guy Endore
     I'M WITH YOU IN ROCKLAND by Jack Dann
     MASKS by Damon Knight
     FORTITUDE by Kurt Vonnegut, Jr.
     NO WOMAN BORN by C. L. Moore
     CAMOUFLAGE by Henry Kuttner
     CRUCIFIXUS ETIAM by Walter M. Miller, Jr.
     PERIOD PIECE by J. J. Coupling
     SOLAR PLEXUS by James Blish
     SEA CHANGE by Thomas N. Scortia
     STARCROSSED by George Zebrowski

     RECOMMENDED READING

25   Souls in Metal: An Anthology of Robot Futures.
        Comp. Mike Ashley. London: Robert Hale;
        New York: St. Martin's Press, 1977. 207pp.

     PREFACE by Mike Ashley

     HELEN O'LOY by Lester del Rey
     --THAT THOU ART MINDFUL OF HIM by Isaac Asimov
     THE TWONKY by Henry Kuttner

The Arts

Business

Catastrophe

29 The End of the World. Ed. Donald A. Wollheim.
    New York: Ace Books, 1956. 159pp. [paper].

    THE YEAR OF THE JACKPOT by Robert A. Heinlein
    LAST NIGHT OF SUMMER by Alfred Coppell
    IMPOSTER by Philip K. Dick
    RESCUE PARTY by Arthur C. Clarke
    OMEGA by Amelia Reynolds Long
    IN THE WORLD'S DUSK by Edmond Hamilton

30 The Earth in Peril. Ed. Donald A. Wollheim.
    New York: Ace Books, 1957. 158pp. [paper].

    THINGS PASS by Murray Leinster
    LETTER FROM THE STARS by A. E. Van Vogt
    THE SILLY SEASON by C. M. Kornbluth
    THE PLANT REVOLT by Edmond Hamilton
    MARY ANONYMOUS by Bryce Walton
    THE STAR by H. G. Wells

Children

(Children of Wonder)
> PART 7: IN TIMES TO COME
> "THE HATCHERY" by Aldous Huxley
> ERRAND BOY by William Tenn
> NIGHTMARE FOR FUTURE REFERENCE: A NARRATIVE
>   POEM by Stephen Vincent Benét [non-fiction]

32 Tomorrow's Children: 18 Tales of Fantasy and
    Science Fiction. Ed. Isaac Asimov. New York:
    Doubleday, 1966. 431pp.

INTRODUCTION by Isaac Asimov

NO LIFE OF THEIR OWN by Clifford D. Simak
THE ACCOUNTANT by Robert Sheckley
NOVICE by James H. Schmitz
CHILD OF VOID by Margaret St. Clair
WHEN THE BOUGH BREAKS by Lewis Padgett
A PAIL OF AIR by Fritz Leiber
JUNIOR ACHIEVEMENT by William Lee
CABIN BOY by Damon Knight
THE LITTLE TERROR by Will F. Jenkins
GILEAD by Zenna Henderson
THE MENACE FROM EARTH by Robert A. Heinlein
THE WAYWARD CRAVAT by Gertrude Friedberg
THE FATHER-THING by Philip K. Dick
STAR, BRIGHT by Mark Clifton
ALL SUMMER IN A DAY by Ray Bradbury
IT'S A GOOD LIFE by Jerome Bixby
THE PLACE OF THE GODS by Stephen Vincent Benét
THE UGLY LITTLE BOY by Isaac Asimov

33 Children of Infinity: Original Science Fiction
    Stories for Young Readers. Ed. Roger Elwood.
    New York: Franklin Watts, 1973. 178pp.

FOREWORD by Roger Elwood
A GAME OF FUTURES--AN INTRODUCTION by Lester
    del Rey

(Children of Infinity)
 TIME BROTHER by Raymond F. Jones
 CONVERSATIONS AT LOTHAR'S by Barry N. Malzberg
 WINGLESS ON AVALON by Póul Anderson
 SPACE-BORN by Robert Bloch
 ALL YOU CAN EAT by Harvey L. and Audrey L.
   Bilker
 OPENING THE DOOR by Philip Jose Farmer
 TERRAFIED by Arthur Tofte
 HALF LIFE by Rachel Cosgrove Payes
 THE TOWER by Thomas N. Scortia
 WAKE UP TO THUNDER by Dean R. Koontz

34 The Other Side of Tomorrow: Original Science
    Fiction Stories About Young People of the Fu-
    ture. Ed. Roger Elwood. New York: Random
    House, 1973. 207pp.

    INTRODUCTION by Roger Elwood

    COME SING THE MOONS OF MORAVENN by Leigh
      Brackett
    EXAMINATION DAY by Gordon Eklund
    THE SPEEDERS by Arthur Tofte
    LET MY PEOPLE GO! by Joseph Green
    NIGHT OF THE MILLENNIUM by Edward D. Hoch
    A BOWL OF BISKIES MAKES A GROWING BOY by
      Raymond F. Jones
    FINAL EXAM by Thomas N. Scortia
    THE OTHERS by J. Hunter Holly
    PEACE, LOVE, AND FOOD FOR THE HUNGRY by Gail
      Kimberly

Christmas

The City

36 <u>Cities of Wonder</u>. Ed. Damon Knight. Garden City: Doubleday, 1966. 252pp.

INTRODUCTION by Damon Knight

SINGLE COMBAT by Robert Abernathy
DUMB WAITER by Walter M. Miller, Jr.
JESTING PILOT by Henry Kuttner
"IT'S GREAT TO BE BACK!" by Robert A. Heinlein
BILLENIUM by J. G. Ballard
OKIE by James Blish
THE LUCKIEST MAN IN DENV by C. M. Kornbluth
THE MACHINE STOPS by E. M. Forster
THE UNDERPRIVILEGED by Brian Aldiss
BY THE WATERS OF BABYLON by Stephen Vincent
  Benét
FORGETFULNESS by Don A. Stuart

37 <u>Future City</u>. Ed. Roger Elwood. New York: Trident Press, 1973. 256pp.

FOREWORD by Clifford D. Simak

IN PRAISE OF NEW YORK by Tom Disch
THE SIGHTSEERS by Ben Bova
MEANWHILE, WE ELIMINATE by Andrew J. Offutt
THINE ALABASTER CITIES GLEAM by Laurence M.
  Janifer
CULTURE LOCK by Barry N. Malzberg
THE WORLD AS WILL AND WALLPAPER by R. A.
  Lafferty
VIOLATION by William F. Nolan

(Future City)
CITY LIGHTS, CITY NIGHTS by K. M. O'Donnell
THE UNDERCITY by Dean R. Koontz
APARTMENT HUNTING by Harvey and Audrey Bilker
AS A DROP by D. M. Price
ABENDLANDES by Virginia Kidd
THE WEARIEST RIVER by Thomas N. Scortia
DEATH OF A CITY by Frank Herbert
ASSASSINS OF AIR by George Zebrowski
GETTING ACROSS by Robert Silverberg
IN DARK PLACES by Joe L. Hensley
REVOLUTION by Robin Schaeffer
CHICAGO by Thomas F. Monteleone
THE MOST PRIMITIVE by Ray Russell
HINDSIGHT: 480 SECONDS by Harlan Ellison
5,000,000 A.D. by Miriam Allen deFord

AFTERWORD by Frederik Pohl

38 Hot & Cold Running Cities: An Anthology of
    Science Fiction. Ed. Georgess McHargue.
    New York: Holt, Rinehart and Winston, 1974.
    245pp.

    [INTRODUCTION by Georgess McHargue]

    ENCHANTED VILLAGE by A. E. Van Vogt
    THE DEEPS by Keith Roberts
    THE MENACE FROM EARTH by Robert A. Heinlein
    METROPOLITAN NIGHTMARE by Stephen Vincent Benét
    THE LUCKIEST MAN IN DENV by C. M. Kornbluth
    THE CITY THAT LOVES YOU by Raymond Banks
    THE PLACE WHERE CHICAGO WAS by James Harmon
    NATURAL STATE by Damon Knight
    PLENITUDE by Will Worthington

39 The City: 2000 A.D. Urban Life Through Science
    Fiction. Ed. Ralph Clem, Martin Harry Greenberg
    and Joseph Olander. New York: Fawcett Crest,
    1976. 304pp. [paper].

The City

(The City)

Corruption

Crime and Punishment

41   <u>The Saint's Choice of Impossible Crime</u>. Ed.
Leslie Charteris. Hollywood, CA: Bond-
Charteris, 1945. 125pp. [paper].

THE GOLD STANDARD by Leslie Charteris
THE IMPOSSIBLE HIGHWAY by Oscar J. Friend
PLANETS MUST SLAY by Frank Belknap Long
DAYMARE by Fredric Brown
TROPHY by Henry Kuttner

42   <u>Space Police</u>. Ed. Andre Norton. Cleveland:
World, 1956. 255pp.

WE POLICE OURSELVES: FUTURE TENSE
BAIT by Roy L. Clough, Jr.
THE CLOSED DOOR by Kendall Foster Crossen
BEEP by James Blish

WE ARE POLICED
OF THOSE WHO CAME by George Longdon
POLICE OPERATION by H. Beam Piper
PAX GALACTICA by Ralph Williams

GALACTIC AGENTS
TOUGH OLD MAN by L. Ron Hubbard
AGENT OF VEGA by James H. Schmitz
THE SUB-STANDARD SARDINES by Jack Vance

43   <u>The Science-Fictional Sherlock Holmes</u>. Ed.
Robert C. Peterson. Denver: The Council of
Four, 1960. 137pp.

(The Science-Fictional Sherlock Holmes)
THE MARTIAN CROWN JEWELS by Poul Anderson
HALF A HOKA-POUL ANDERSON by Gordon R. Dickson
THE ADVENTURE OF THE MISPLACED HOUND by Poul
    Anderson and Gordon R. Dickson
THE ANOMALY OF THE EMPTY MAN by Anthony Boucher
THE GREATEST TERTIAN by Anthony Boucher
THE ADVENTURE OF THE SNITCH IN TIME by Mack
    Reynolds and August Derleth
THE ADVENTURE OF THE BALL OF NOSTRADAMUS by
    Mack Reynolds and August Derleth
THE RETURN by H. Beam Piper and John J. McGuire

44   Space, Time & Crime. Ed. Miriam Allen deFord.
     New York: Paperback Library, 1964. 174pp.
     [paper].

     INTRODUCTION by Miriam Allen deFord

     CRISIS, 1999 by Fredric Brown
     CRIMINAL NEGLIGENCE by J. Francis McComas
     THE TALKING STONE by Isaac Asimov
     THE PAST AND ITS DEAD PEOPLE by R. Bretnor
     THE ADVENTURE OF THE SNITCH IN TIME by Mack
         Reynolds and August Derleth
     THE EYES HAVE IT by James McKimmey
     PUBLIC EYE by Anthony Boucher
     THE INNOCENT ARRIVAL by Poul and Karen Anderson
     THIRD OFFENSE by Frederik Pohl
     THE RECURRENT SUITOR by Ron Goulart
     TRY AND CHANGE THE PAST by Fritz Leiber
     ROPE'S END by Miriam Allen deFord
     OR THE GRASSES GROW by Avram Davidson

45   Crime Prevention in the 30th Century. Ed. Hans
     Stefan Santesson. New York: Walker, 1969.
     175pp.

     INTRODUCTION by Hans Stefan Santesson

     JACK FELL DOWN by John Brunner
     THE EEL by Miriam Allen deFord

(Crime Prevention in the 30th Century)
THE FUTURE IS OURS by Stephen Dentinger
VELVET GLOVE by Harry Harrison
LET THERE BE LIGHT! by Morris Hershman
COMPUTER COPS by Edward D. Hoch
APPLE by Anne McCaffrey
RAIN CHECK by Judith Merril
TOYS by Tom Purdom
PARTY OF THE TWO PARTS by William Tenn

46   Dark Sins, Dark Dreams: Crime in Science Fiction.
      Ed. Barry N. Malzberg and Bill Pronzini. Garden
      City: Doubleday, 1978. 224pp.

      INTRODUCTION by Bill Pronzini

      THE BIOGRAPHY PROJECT by H. L. Gold
      A MAN TO MY WOUNDING by Poul Anderson
      THE WINNER by Donald E. Westlake
      BOOTH 13 by John Lutz
      THE WOLFRAM HUNTERS by Edward D. Hoch
      TO SEE THE INVISIBLE MAN by Robert Silverberg
      THE MAN WHO COLLECTED "THE SHADOW" by Bill
        Pronzini
      BERNIE THE FAUST by William Tenn
      THE FIRE MAN by Elizabeth A. Lynn
      NON SUB HOMINE by H. W. Whyte
      MURDER, 2090 by C. B. Gilford
      THE GENERALISSIMO'S BUTTERFLY by Chelsea Quinn
        Yarbro
      THE SEVERAL MURDERS OF ROGER AKROYD by Barry N.
        Malzberg
      VIEW, WITH A DIFFERENCE by C. L. Grant
      THE EXECUTIONER by A. J. Budrys

      AFTERWORD: OF CRIME AND SCIENCE FICTION by
        Barry N. Malzberg

Dimensions (Other)

47 <u>Science Fiction Adventures in Dimension</u>. Ed.
Groff Conklin. New York: Vanguard Press, 1953.
354pp.

PART ONE: TIME TALES

PRESENT TO FUTURE
YESTERDAY WAS MONDAY by Theodore Sturgeon
AMBITION by William L. Bade
THE MIDDLE OF THE WEEK AFTER NEXT by Murray
  Leinster
...AND IT COMES OUT HERE by Lester del Rey

PRESENT TO PAST
CASTAWAY by A. Bertram Chandler
THE GOOD PROVIDER by Marion Gross
REVERSE PHYLOGENY by Amelia R. Long
OTHER TRACKS by William Sell

PAST TO PRESENT
"WHAT SO PROUDLY WE HAIL..." by Day Keene
NIGHT MEETING by Ray Bradbury

FUTURE TO PRESENT
PERFECT MURDER by H. L. Gold
THE FLIGHT THAT FAILED by E. Mayne Hull
ENDOWMENT POLICY by Lewis Padgett
PETE CAN FIX IT by Raymond F. Jones

PART TWO: PARALLEL WORLDS

THE MIST by Peter Cartur
THE GOSTAK AND THE DOSHES by Miles J. Breuer,
  M.D.

(Science Fiction Adventures in Dimension)
WHAT IF... by Isaac Asimov
RING AROUND THE REDHEAD by John D. MacDonald
TIGER BY THE TAIL by Allan E. Nourse
WAY OF ESCAPE by William F. Temple
SUBURBAN FRONTIERS by Roger Flint Young
BUSINESS OF KILLING by Fritz Leiber, Jr.
TO FOLLOW KNOWLEDGE by Frank Belknap Long, Jr.

48   Other Dimensions: Ten Stories of Science Fiction.
      Ed. Robert Silverberg. New York: Hawthorn
      Books, 1973. 178pp.

      ACKNOWLEDGMENTS
      INTRODUCTION by Robert Silverberg

      --AND HE BUILT A CROOKED HOUSE by Robert A.
        Heinlein
      NARROW VALLEY by R. A. Lafferty
      WALL OF DARKNESS by Arthur C. Clarke
      THE DESTINY OF MILTON GOMRATH by Alexei Panshin
      STANLEY TOOTHBRUSH by Terry Carr
      INSIDE by Carol Carr
      THE CAPTURED CROSS-SECTION by Miles J. Breuer,
        M.D.
      MUGWUMP by Robert Silverberg
      THE WORLDS OF IF by Stanley G. Weinbaum
      DISAPPEARING ACT by Alfred Bester

Drugs

49 <u>Dream Trips</u>: <u>Stories of Weird and Unearthly</u>
<u>Drugs</u>. Ed. Michel Parry. UK: Panther Books,
1974. 160pp. [paper].

INTRODUCTION by Michel Parry

THE HASHISH MAN by Lord Dunsany
AS DREAMS ARE MADE ON by Joseph F. Pumilia
THE ADVENTURES OF THE PIPE by Richard Marsh
DREAM–DUST FROM MARS by Manly Wade Wellman
THE LIFE SERUM by Paul S. Powers
MORNING AFTER by Robert Sheckley
UNDER THE KNIFE by H. G. Wells
THE GOOD TRIP by Ursula K. Le Guin
NO DIRECTION HOME by Norman Spinrad
THE PHANTOM DRUG by A. W. Kapfer

50 <u>Strange Ecstasies</u>. Ed. Michel Parry. New York:
Pinnacle Books, 1974. 179pp. [paper]

INTRODUCTION by Michel Parry

THE PLUTONIAN DRUG by Clark Ashton Smith
THE DREAM PILLS by F. H. Davis
THE WHITE POWDER by Arthur Machen
THE NEW ACCELERATOR by H. G. Wells
THE BIG FIX by Richard Wilson
THE SECRET SONGS by Fritz Leiber
THE HOUNDS OF TINDALOS by Frank Belknap Long
SUBJECTIVITY by Norman Spinrad
WHAT TO DO UNTIL THE ANALYST COMES by Frederik
  Pohl
PIPE DREAM by Chris Miller

Dystopia

51 <u>Man Against Tomorrow</u>. Ed. William F. Nolan.
   New York: Avon Books, 1965. 191pp. [paper].

   INTRODUCTION by William F. Nolan

   SPECIAL DELIVERY by Kris Neville
   THE ROOM by Ray Russell
   AFTER THE SIRENS by Hugh Hood
   I, DREAMER by Walter M. Miller, Jr.
   PAYMENT IN FULL by Ray Bradbury
   SEVENTH VICTIM by Robert Sheckley
   BIRTHDAY PRESENT by Charles E. Fritch
   TRANSFORMER by Chad Oliver
   MASS FOR MIXED VOICES by Charles Beaumont
   THE FREEWAY by George Clayton Johnson
   NOBODY STARVES by Ron Goulart
   AND MILES TO GO BEFORE I SLEEP by William F.
      Nolan

52 <u>Dark Stars</u>. Ed. Robert Silverberg. New York:
   Ballantine Books, 1969. 309pp. [paper].

   INTRODUCTION by Robert Silverberg

   SHARK SHIP by C. M. Kornbluth
   POLITY AND CUSTOM OF THE CAMIROI by R. A.
      Lafferty
   COMING—OF—AGE DAY by A. K. Jorgensson
   HERESIES OF THE HUGE GOD by Brian W. Aldiss
   THE STREETS OF ASHKALON by Harry Harrison
   THE TOTALLY RICH by John Brunner
   IMPOSTOR by Philip K. Dick

(Dark Stars)
    ROAD TO NIGHTFALL by Robert Silverberg
    THE BEAST THAT SHOUTED LOVE AT THE HEART OF THE
        WORLD by Harlan Ellison
    PSYCHOSMOSIS by David I. Masson
    THE CAGE OF SAND by J. G. Ballard
    A DESKFUL OF GIRLS by Fritz Leiber
    ON THE ALL OF THE LODGE by James Blish and
        Virginia Kidd
    MASKS by Damon Knight
    KEEPERS OF THE HOUSE by Lester del Rey
    JOURNEY'S END by Poul Anderson

53   Science Against Man. Ed. Anthony Cheetham.
     New York: Avon Books, 1970. 221pp. [paper].

     INTRODUCTION by Anthony Cheetham

     THE LOST CONTINENT by Norman Spinrad
     IN THE BEGINNING by Robert Silverberg
     THE HUNTER AT HIS EASE by Brian Aldiss
     MAN'S ESTATE by Paul Ableman
     HAROLD WILSON AT THE COSMIC COCKTAIL PARTY by
         Bob Shaw
     STATISTICIAN'S DAY by James Blish
     THE INVISIBLE IDIOT by John Brunner
     SMALL MOUTH, BAD TASTE by Piers Anthony
     THE EVER BRANCHING TREE by Harry Harrison
     SEA WOLVES by Michael Moorcock
     THE PENULTIMATE TRIP by Andrew Travers

54   The Ruins of Earth: An Anthology of the Immediate
     Future. Ed. Thomas M. Disch. New York: G. P.
     Putnam's Sons, 1971. 279pp.

     INTRODUCTION: ON SAVING THE WORLD by Thomas M.
         Disch

         THE WAY IT IS:
     DEER IN THE WORKS by Kurt Vonnegut, Jr.
     THREE MILLION SQUARE MILES by Gene Wolfe
     CLOSING WITH NATURE by Norman Rush

(The Ruins of Earth)

    WHY IT IS THE WAY IT IS:
THE PLOT TO SAVE THE WORLD by Michael Brownstein
AUTOFAC by Philip K. Dick
ROOMMATES by Harry Harrison
GROANING HINGES OF THE WORLD by R. A. Lafferty

    HOW IT COULD GET WORSE:
GAS MASK by James D. Houston
WEDNESDAY, NOVEMBER 15, 1967 by Geo. Alec
  Effinger
THE CAGE OF SAND by J. G. Ballard
ACCIDENT VERTIGO by Kenwood Elmslie
THE BIRDS by Daphne du Maurier

    UNFORTUNATE SOLUTIONS:
DO IT FOR MAMA! by Jerrold J. Mundis
THE DREADFUL HAS ALREADY HAPPENED by Norman
  Kagan
THE SHAKER REVIVAL by Gerald Jonas
AMERICA THE BEAUTIFUL by Fritz Leiber

55   Dystopian Visions. Ed. Roger Elwood. Englewood
     Cliffs, NJ: Prentice-Hall, 1975. 197pp.

INTRODUCTION by Roger Elwood

    THE RIGHT TO LIFE
BREATH'S A WARE THAT WILL NOT KEEP by Thomas F.
  Monteleone
COME TAKE A DIP WITH ME IN THE GENETIC POOL by
  Rachel Cosgrove Payes

    ANOMIE
UNCOUPLING by Barry N. Malzberg
FACES FORWARD by Jack Dann and George Zebrowski

    THE ROOTS OF VIOLENCE
CIVIS LAPVTVS SVM by Gene Wolfe
WEAPONS by Pamela Sargent and George Zebrowski

(Dystopian Visions)

    PREJUDICE
A DEATH IN COVENTRY by Joseph Green
OR LITTLE DUCKS EACH DAY by R. A. Lafferty

    OLD AGE
CIVIS OBIT by Laurence M. Janifer
WHERE SUMMER SONG RINGS HOLLOW by Gail Kimberly

    SEX
GOING DOWN by Barry N. Malzberg
THE GIFT by Laurence M. Janifer

    CULTURE SHOCK
XENOFREAK/XENOPHOBE by Edward Bryant

√ 56   <u>Earth In Transit</u>: <u>Science Fiction and Contempo-</u>
    <u>rary Problems</u>. Ed. Sheila Schwartz. New York:
    Dell, 1976. 271pp. [paper].

INTRODUCTION by Sheila Schwartz

    I. UTOPIA OR DYSTOPIA?
LOT by Ward Moore
HISTORY LESSON by Arthur C. Clarke
TO SEE THE INVISIBLE MAN by Robert Silverberg
MODUS VIVENDI by Walter Bupp

    II. OVERPOPULATION IN DYSTOPIA
ROOMMATES by Harry Harrison
A HAPPY DAY IN 2381 by Robert Silverberg
BILLENIUM by J. G. Ballard
SOUNDLESS EVENING by Lee Hoffman

    III. THOUGHT CONTROL IN DYSTOPIA
THE WINNER by Donald E. Westlake
I TELL YOU, IT'S TRUE by Poul Anderson
WE CAN REMEMBER IT FOR YOU WHOLESALE by Philip
    K. Dick
THE SUBLIMINAL MAN by J. G. Ballard

(Earth in Transit)

    IV. MACHINE POWER IN DYSTOPIA
I MADE YOU by Walter M. Miller, Jr.
CITY OF YESTERDAY by Terry Carr
HEMEAC by E. G. Von Wald

57   <u>The Late Great Future</u>. Ed. Gregory Fitz Gerald
and John Dillon. Greenwich, CT: Fawcett Crest,
1976. 288pp. [paper].

INTRODUCTION by Gregory Fitz Gerald and John
   Dillon

WHEN WE WENT TO SEE THE END OF THE WORLD by
   Robert Silverberg
A THING OF CUSTOM by L. Sprague de Camp
THE PEDESTRIAN by Ray Bradbury
WILLIAM AND MARY by Roald Dahl
FLOWERS FOR ALGERNON by Daniel Keyes
THE COUNTRY OF THE KIND by Damon Knight
COME TO VENUS MELANCHOLY by Thomas M. Disch
HOW BEAUTIFUL WITH BANNERS by James Blish
THE TOTALLY RICH by John Brunner
AMERICA THE BEAUTIFUL by Fritz Leiber
THE ANNEX by John D. MacDonald
THE SHODDY LANDS by C. S. Lewis
CRUCIFIXUS ETIAM by Walter M. Miller, Jr.
THREE PORTRAITS AND A PRAYER by Frederik Pohl

Ecology

58 Nightmare Age. Ed. Frederik Pohl. New York:
    Ballantine Books, 1970. 312pp. [paper].

    ECO-CATASTROPHE! by Paul R. Ehrlich
    UNCALCULATED RISK by Christopher Anvil
    THE CENSUS TAKERS by Frederik Pohl
    THE MARCHING MORONS by C. M. Kornbluth
    A BAD DAY FOR SALES by Fritz Leiber
    STATION HR972 by Kenneth Bulmer
    X MARKS THE PEDWALK by Fritz Leiber
    DAY OF TRUCE by Clifford D. Simak
    AMONG THE BAD BABOONS by Mack Reynolds
    THE LUCKIEST MAN IN DENV by C. M. Kornbluth
    THE MIDAS PLAGUE by Frederik Pohl
    NEW APPLES IN THE GARDEN by Kris Neville
    THE YEAR OF THE JACKPOT by Robert A. Heinlein

59 Saving Worlds: A Collection of Original Science
    Fiction Stories. Ed. Roger Elwood and Virginia
    Kidd. Garden City: Doubleday, 1973. 237pp.

    INTRODUCTION by Frank Herbert

    SAVING THE WORLD by Terry Carr
    PARKS OF REST AND CULTURE by George Zebrowski
    THE QUALITY OF THE PRODUCT by Lil & Kris Neville
    TWO POEMS by Tom Disch [poetry]
    SMALL WAR by Katherine MacLean
    DESIRABLE LAKESIDE RESIDENCE by Andre Norton
    THE SMOKEY THE BEAR SUTRA by Gary Snyder
    AN ARTICLE ABOUT HUNTING by Gene Wolfe
    NOONDAY DEVIL by Dennis O'Neil

(Saving Worlds)
SCORNER'S SEAT by R. A. Lafferty
THE BATTERED-EARTH SYNDROME by Barry N. Malzberg
WINDMILL by Poul Anderson
PARADISE REGAINED by Cogswell Thomas
BEAUTYLAND by Gene Wolfe
THE DAY by Colin Saxton
TWO POEMS by D. M. Price [poetry]
DON'T HOLD YOUR BREATH by A. E. Van Vogt
THE WIND AND THE RAIN by Robert Silverberg

60   The Infinite Web: Eight Stories of Science Fic-
      tion. Ed. Robert Silverberg. New York: Dial
      Press, 1977. 239pp.

      INTRODUCTION by Robert Silverberg

      GRANDPA by James H. Schmitz
      OF MIST, AND GRASS, AND SAND by Vonda M.
        McIntyre
      THERE IS A TIDE by Brian W. Aldiss
      THE DEEP RANGE by Arthur C. Clarke
      THE WORLD BETWEEN by Jack Vance
      ENCASED IN ANCIENT RIND by R. A. Lafferty
      ON THE LAST AFTERNOON by James Tiptree, Jr.
      THE WIND AND THE RAIN by Robert Silverberg

Education

Education

Empires (Galactic)

63   <u>Galactic Empires</u>: <u>Volume II</u>. Ed. Brian W.
     Aldiss. London: Weidenfeld & Nicolson, 1976.
     296pp.

INTRODUCTION by Brian W. Aldiss

Section 2: MATURITY OR BUST (continued)

    i.   'You Can't Impose Civilization by
        Force'
ESCAPE TO CHAOS by John Macdonald
CONCEALMENT by A. E. Van Vogt
TO CIVILIZE by Algis Budrys
BEEP by James Blish

    ii.   The Other End of the Stick
DOWN THE RIVER by Mack Reynolds
THE BOUNTY HUNTER by Avram Davidson
NOT YET THE END by Fredric Brown

Section 3 DECLINE AND FALL

    i.   All Things Are Cyclic
TONIGHT THE STARS REVOLT! by Gardner F. Fox
FINAL ENCOUNTER by Harry Harrison

    ii.   Big Ancestors and Descendants
LORD OF A THOUSAND SONS by Poul Anderson
BIG ANCESTOR by F. L. Wallace
THE INTERLOPERS by Roger Dee

EPILOGUE by Brian W. Aldiss

Ethics

Freedom

65   <u>The Liberated Future</u>.   Ed. Robert Hoskins.
      Greenwich, CT: Fawcett Crest, 1974.   304pp.
      [paper].

INTRODUCTION by Robert Hoskins

SAM HALL by Poul Anderson
ENCASED IN ANCIENT RIND by R. A. Lafferty
THE LITTLE BLACK BAG by C. M. Kornbluth
THE TROUBLE WITH EARTH PEOPLE by Katherine
   MacLean
STREET OF DREAMS, FEET OF CLAY by Robert
   Sheckley
PRIVATE EYE by Henry Kuttner
SOFT COME THE DRAGONS by Dean R. Koontz
THE RUN FROM HOME by Joe L. Hensley
CONVERSATIONS AT LOTHAR'S by Barry N. Malzberg
A MEETING OF MINDS by Anne McCaffrey
THE LIBERATION OF EARTH by William Tenn
A TRIP TO THE HEAD by Ursula K. Le Guin

Friendship

Government

(American Government Through Science Fiction)
THE ASSASSINATION OF JOHN FITZGERALD KENNEDY
CONSIDERED AS A DOWNHILL MOTOR RACE by J. G.
Ballard

SELECTED BIBLIOGRAPHY

68   Political Science Fiction. Ed. Martin Harry
Greenberg and Patricia S. Warrick. Englewood
Cliffs, NJ: Prentice-Hall, 1974. 415pp.

PREFACE by Martin Harry Greenberg and Patricia
S. Warrick
INTRODUCTION by Martin Harry Greenberg and
Patricia S. Warrick

I.   IDEOLOGY AND POLITICAL PHILOSOPHY
FREEDOM by Mack Reynolds
REMEMBER THE ALAMO! by R. R. Fehrenbach
DISAPPEARING ACT by Alfred Bester
THE LAST OF THE DELIVERERS by Poul Anderson

II.   POLITICAL LEADERSHIP
CALL HIM LORD by Gordon R. Dickson
THE SHORT ONES by Raymond E. Banks
ADRIFT ON THE POLICY LEVEL by Chandler Davis
ETERNITY LOST by Clifford Simak
DEATH AND THE SENATOR by Arthur C. Clarke

III.   ELECTIONS AND ELECTORAL BEHAVIOR
EVIDENCE by Isaac Asimov
FRANCHISE by Isaac Asimov
BEYOND DOUBT by Lyle Monroe and Elma Wentz
2066: ELECTION DAY by Michael Shaara

IV.   POLITICAL VIOLENCE AND REVOLUTION
"REPENT HARLEQUIN," SAID THE TICKTOCKMAN by
Harlan Ellison
BURNING QUESTION by Brian W. Aldiss
...NOT A PRISON MAKE by Joseph P. Martino
THE GENERAL ZAPPED AN ANGEL by Howard Fast

Government

History

INTRODUCTION by Daniel Roselle

   TOPIC 1: PREHISTORIC TIMES
A SOUND OF THUNDER by Ray Bradbury

   TOPIC 2: THE ANCIENT GREEKS
THE GORGON'S HEAD by Gertrude Bacon

   TOPIC 3: THE AGE OF CHARLEMAGNE
THUS WE FRUSTRATE CHARLEMAGNE by R. A. Lafferty

   TOPIC 4: THE RENAISSANCE
THE SMILE by Ray Bradbury

   TOPIC 5: RELATIONS BETWEEN EAST AND WEST
THE MAN ON TOP by R. Bretnor

   TOPIC 6: EXPANDING HORIZONS OF SCIENCE
IT'S SUCH A BEAUTIFUL DAY by Isaac Asimov

   TOPIC 7: RISE OF MODERN DICTATORS
I KILL MYSELF by Julian Kawalec

   TOPIC 8: ATOMIC BOMBS AND RADIATIONS
THAT ONLY A MOTHER by Judith Merril

   TOPIC 9: OUR CONTEMPORARY WORLD--PROBLEMS
        AND ISSUES

   A. WOMEN'S LIBERATION
SURVIVAL SHIP by Judith Merril

(Transformations)

  B. GENERATION GAP
ABSALOM by Henry Kuttner

  C. DEHUMANIZATION
"REPENT, HARLEQUIN!" SAID THE TICKTOCKMAN by
Harlan Ellison

70 Transformations II: Understanding American History Through Science Fiction. Ed. Daniel
  Roselle. Greenwich, CT: Fawcett Crest, 1974.
  143pp. [paper].

INTRODUCTION by Daniel Roselle

  TOPIC 1: METHODS OF HISTORIANS
HISTORY LESSON by Arthur C. Clarke

  TOPIC 2: EXPLORATION AND DISCOVERY
THE CONQUEST OF THE MOON by Washington Irving

  TOPIC 3: SPIRITS OF 1776
I DO NOT HEAR YOU, SIR by Avram Davidson

  TOPIC 4: THE TEXAS REVOLUTION
REMEMBER THE ALAMO by T. R. Fehrenbach

  TOPIC 5: THE WAR BETWEEN THE STATES
THE DRUMMER BOY OF SHILOH by Ray Bradbury

  TOPIC 6: EARLY TWENTIETH-CENTURY AMERICA
A SCENT OF SARSAPARILLA by Ray Bradbury

  TOPIC 7: WORLD WAR I
TRANSLATION ERROR by Robert Silverberg

  TOPIC 8: OUR CONTEMPORARY WORLD: PROBLEMS
  AND ISSUES

  A. EDUCATION AND THE STUDENT
BEYOND THE GAME by Vance Aandahl

  B. COMPUTERS AND HUMAN BEINGS
COMPUTERS DON'T ARGUE by Gordon R. Dickson

<u>(Transformations II)</u>

        C.   END OF CIVILIZATION
THE PORTABLE PHONOGRAPH by Walter Van Tilburg
  Clark

Humor

(Never in This World)
REBEL by Ward Moore
SENHOR ZUMBEIRA'S LEG by Félix Martí-Ibañez
OR ELSE by Henry Kuttner and C. L. Moore
CRITIQUE OF IMPURE REASON by Poul Anderson

73   Cosmic Laughter: Science Fiction For the Fun Of
     It. Comp. Joe Haldeman. New York: Holt,
     Rinehart and Winston, 1974. 189pp.

     INTRODUCTION by Joe Haldeman

     A SLIGHT MISCALCULATION by Ben Bova
     "IT'S A BIRD! IT'S A PLANE!" by Norman Spinrad
     THE ROBOTS ARE HERE by Terry Carr
     I OF NEWTON by Joe Haldeman
     THE MEN WHO MURDERED MOHAMMED by Alfred Bester
     TO SERVE MAN by Damon Knight
     THE BOMB IN THE BATHTUB by Thomas N. Scortia
     THE BLACK SORCERER OF THE BLACK CASTLE by
        Andrew J. Offutt
     GALLEGHER PLUS by Henry Kuttner

74   Infinite Jests: The Lighter Side of Science Fic-
     tion. Ed. Robert Silverberg. Radnor, PA:
     Chilton, 1974. 231pp.

     INTRODUCTION by Robert Silverberg

     VENUS AND THE SEVEN SEXES by William Tenn
     BABEL II by Damon Knight
     USEFUL PHRASES FOR THE TOURIST by Joanna Russ
     CONVERSATIONAL MODE by Grahame Leman
     HERESIES OF THE HUGE GOD by Brian W. Aldiss
     (NOW +n), (NOW -n) by Robert Silverberg
     SLOW TUESDAY NIGHT by R. A. Lafferty
     HELP! I AM DR. MORRIS GOLDPEPPER by
        Avram Davidson
     OH, TO BE A BLOBEL! by Philip K. Dick
     HOBSON'S CHOICE by Alfred Bester
     I PLINGLOT, WHO YOU? by Frederik Pohl

75 Antigrav: <u>Cosmic Comedies by SF Masters</u>. Ed.
    Philip Strick. New York: Taplinger, 1976.
    184pp.

INTRODUCTION by Philip Strick

SPACE RATS OF THE C.C.C. by Harry Harrison
HOW THE WORLD WAS SAVED by Stanislaw Lem
IT WAS NOTHING—REALLY! by Theodore Sturgeon
THE GLITCH by James Blish (with L. Jerome
    Stanton)
CONVERSATIONS ON A STARSHIP IN WARPDRIVE by
    John Brosnan
THE ALIBI MACHINE by Larry Niven
EMERGENCY SOCIETY by Uta Frith
LOOK, YOU THINK YOU'VE GOT TROUBLES? by Carol
    Carr
A DELIGHTFUL COMEDIC PREMISE by Barry N.
    Malzberg
TROLLS by Robert Borski
ELEPHANT WITH WOODEN LEG by John Sladek
PLANTING TIME by Pete Adams and Charles
    Nightingale
BY THE SEASHORE by R. A. Lafferty
HARDCASTLE by Ron Goulart
THE ERGOT SHOW by Brian W. Aldiss

Invasion

77　Gentle Invaders.　Ed. Hans Stefan Santesson.
　　New York:　Belmont Books, 1969.　176pp.　[paper].

　　INTRODUCTION by Hans Stefan Santesson

　　SIT BY THE FIRE by Myrle Benedict
　　THE QUEER ONES by Leigh Brackett
　　FREAK SHOW by Miriam Allen deFord
　　SUBCOMMITTEE by Zenna Henderson
　　UNNATURAL ACT by Edward D. Hoch
　　THE NIGHT HE CRIED by Fritz Leiber
　　THE MARTIANS AND THE COYS by Mack Reynolds
　　QUIZ GAME by Frank M. Robinson
　　DEAR DEVIL by Eric Frank Russell
　　PARTY OF THE TWO PARTS by William Tenn

78　Invaders From Space:　Ten Stories of Science Fic-
　　tion.　Ed. Robert Silverberg.　New York:
　　Hawthorn, 1972.　241pp.

　　INTRODUCTION by Robert Silverberg

　　THE LIBERATION OF EARTH by William Tenn
　　THE SILLY SEASON by C. M. Kornbluth
　　ROOG by Philip K. Dick
　　NIGHTWINGS by Robert Silverberg
　　NOBODY SAW THE SHIP by Murray Leinster
　　STORM WARNING by Donald A. Wollheim
　　CATCH THAT MARTIAN by Damon Knight
　　RESURRECTION by A. E. Van Vogt
　　PICTURES DON'T LIE by Katherine MacLean
　　HERESIES OF THE HUGE GOD by Brian W. Aldiss

Invisibility

THE WEISSENBROCH SPECTACLES by L. Sprague de Camp and Fletcher Pratt
THE SHADOW AND THE FLASH by Jack London
THE NEW ACCELERATOR by H. G. Wells
INVISIBLE BOY by Ray Bradbury
THE INVISIBLE PRISONER by Maurice LeBlanc
LOVE IN THE DARK by H. L. Gold
WHAT WAS IT? by Fitz-James O'Brien
THE INVISIBLE DOVE DANCER OF STRATHPHEEN ISLAND by John Collier
THE VANISHING AMERICAN by Charles Beaumont
SHOTTLE BOP by Theodore Sturgeon
THE INVISIBLE MAN MURDER CASE by Henry Slesar

Jewishness

80 <u>Wandering Stars</u>: <u>An Anthology of Jewish Fantasy</u>
     <u>and Science Fiction</u>. Ed. Jack Dann. New York:
     Harper & Row, 1974. 243pp.

INTRODUCTION: WHY ME? by Isaac Asimov
ON VENUS, HAVE WE GOT A RABBI by William Tenn
THE GOLEM by Avram Davidson
UNTO THE FOURTH GENERATION by Isaac Asimov
LOOK, YOU THINK YOU'VE GOT TROUBLES by Carol
     Carr
GOSLIN DAY by Avram Davidson
THE DYBBUK OF MAZEL TOV IV by Robert Silverberg
TROUBLE WITH WATER by H. L. Gold
GATHER BLUE ROSES by Pamela Sargent
THE JEWBIRD by Bernard Malamud
PARADISE LOST by Geo. Alec Effinger
STREET OF DREAMS, FEET OF CLAY by Robert
     Sheckley
JACHID AND JECHIDAH by Isaac Bashevis Singer
I'M LOOKING FOR KADAK by Harlan Ellison

Machines

83   Beyond Control: Seven Stories of Science Fiction.
     Ed. Robert Silverberg. Nashville: Thomas
     Nelson, 1972. 219pp.

     INTRODUCTION by Robert Silverberg

     CHILD'S PLAY by William Tenn
     AUTOFAC by Philip K. Dick
     ADAM AND NO EVE by Alfred Bester
     CITY OF YESTERDAY by Terry Carr
     THE IRON CHANCELLOR by Robert Silverberg
     THE BOX by James Blish
     THE DEAD PAST by Isaac Asimov

84   Computers, Computers, Computers: In Fiction and
     in Verse. Ed. D. Van Tassel. Nashville:
     Thomas Nelson, 1977. 192pp.

     MAKE WAY FOR THE MACHINES [Introduction] by
         Dennie L. Van Tassel
     ANSWER by Fredric Brown
     THE PERFECT CRIME by Richard T. Sandberg
     PUT YOUR BRAINS IN YOUR POCKET by Arthur W.
         Hoppe [commentary]
     FOOL'S MATE by Robert T. Sheckley
     POOLING INFORMATION WITH A COMPUTER by Art
         Buchwald [commentary]
     SPACE TO MOVE by Joseph Green
     COMPUTERS DON'T ARGUE by Gordon R. Dickson
     THAT DINKUM THINKUM by Robert A. Heinlein
     ARTHUR'S NIGHT OUT by Laurence Lerner [verse]
     2066: ELECTION DAY by Michael Shaara
     FROM AN ECCLESIASTICAL CHRONICLE by John
         Heath-Stubbs [verse]
     ANSWER "AFFIRMATIVE" OR "NEGATIVE" by Barbara
         Paul
     THE METRIC PLOT by Jim Haynes [commentary]
     PUSH THE MAGIC BUTTON by Renn Zaphiropoulos
         [verse]
     WHEN THE COMPUTER WENT OUT TO LAUNCH by Art
         Buchwald [commentary]

(<u>Computers, Computers, Computers</u>)
    CRIMINAL IN UTOPIA by Mack Reynolds
    THE UNION FOREVER by Barry N. Malzberg
    THE DAY THE COMPUTERS GOT WALDON ASHENFELTER
      by Bob Elliott and Ray Goulding

85   <u>Inside Information</u>: <u>Computers in Fiction</u>. Ed.
     Abbe Mowshowitz. Reading, MA: Addison-Wesley,
     1977. 345pp. [paper].

    ACKNOWLEDGEMENTS
    PREFACE by Abbe Mowshowitz

        Part 1. The New Dispensation
    ALL WATCHED OVER BY MACHINES OF LOVING GRACE
      by Richard Brautigan
    From THE MOON IS A HARSH MISTRESS [novel] by
      Robert Heinlein
    From THE JAGGED ORBIT [novel] by John Bruner
    From PLAYER PIANO by Kurt Vonnegut, Jr.
    From JOURNEY BEYOND TOMORROW by Robert Sheckley
    REPORT by Donald Barthelme

        Part 2. Information and Power
    THE NINE BILLION NAMES OF GOD by Arthur C.
      Clarke
    WHAT'S THE NAME OF THAT TOWN by R. A. Lafferty
    From GILES GOAT-BOY [novel] by John Barth
    THE ANSWER by Fredric Brown

        Part 3. Clockwork Society
    From A MODERN UTOPIA [novel] by H. G. Wells
    EXAMINATION DAY by Henry Slesar
    From THIS PERFECT DAY by Ira Levin
    From THE CITY AND THE STARS by Arthur C. Clarke
    WALTER PERKINS IS HERE! by Raymond E. Banks

        Part 4. Responsibility and Decision-Making
    NOBODY LIVES ON BURTON STREET by Gregory Benford
    From THE STEEL CROCODILE [novel] by D. G.
      Compton

Machines

Machines

(<u>Inside Information</u>)

Mutation

Mutation

(<u>Mutants</u>)

   TOMORROW'S CHILDREN by Poul Anderson and F. N.
     Waldrop
   IT'S A <u>GOOD</u> LIFE by Jerome Bixby
   THE MUTE QUESTION by Forrest J. Ackerman
   LET THE ANTS TRY by Frederik Pohl
   THE CONQUEROR by Mark Clifton
   LIQUID LIFE by Ralph Milne Farley
   HOTHOUSE by Brian W. Aldiss
   OZYMANDIAS by Terry Carr
   THE MAN WHO NEVER FORGOT by Robert Silverberg
   GINNY WRAPPED IN THE SUN by R. A. Lafferty
   WATERSHED by James Blish

Mythology

Overpopulation

Overpopulation

Politics

90 Rulers of Men. Ed. Hans Stefan Santesson.
New York: Pyramid Books, 1965. 173pp.
[paper].

INTRODUCTION by Hans Stefan Santesson

A WAY OF LIFE by Robert Bloch
BE OF GOOD CHEER by Fritz Leiber
THIS EARTH OF MAJESTY by Arthur C. Clarke
A THING OF CUSTOM by L. Sprague de Camp
PRISON BREAK by Miriam Allen deFord
THE EYES HAVE IT by Randall Garrett
MURDERER'S CHAIN by Wenzell Brown
FALL OF KNIGHT by Bertram Chandler
THE K-FACTOR by Harry Harrison
THE WOLFRAM HUNTERS by Edward D. Hoch

91 Bad Moon Rising. Ed. Thomas M. Disch. New York:
Harper & Row, 1973. 302pp.

INTRODUCTION: ON THE ROAD TO 1984 by Thomas M.
Disch

HO CHI MINH ELEGY by Peter Schjeldahl [non-
fiction]
ELEGY FOR JANIS JOPLIN by Marilyn Hacker [non-
fiction]
WE ARE DAINTY LITTLE PEOPLE by Charles Naylor
STRANGERS by Carol Emshwiller
RELATIVES by Geo. Alec Effinger
RIDING by Norman Rush
AN APOCALYPSE: SOME SCENES FROM EUROPEAN LIFE
by Michael Moorcock

Politics

(Bad Moon Rising)
THE WHIMPER OF WHIPPED DOGS by Harlan Ellison
THE GREAT WALL OF MEXICO by John Sladek
THE VILLAGE by Kate Wilhelm
IN BEHALF OF THE PRODUCT by Kit Reed
HOUR OF TRUST by Gene Wolfe
FIGHTING FASCISM by Norman Rush
COLD TURKEY by Ron Padgett and Dick Gallup
WHERE HAVE ALL THE FOLLOWERS GONE? by Raylyn
   Moore
AN OUTLINE OF HISTORY by Malcolm Braly
TWO SADNESSES by Geo. Alec Effinger
EVERYDAY LIFE IN THE LATER ROMAN EMPIRE by
   Thomas M. Disch
UNTOWARD OCCURRENCE AT EMBASSY POETRY READING
   by Marilyn Hacker
FOR APOLLO 11 by Peter Schjeldahl
SOME NOTES ON THE PREDYNASTIC EPOCH by Robert
   Silverberg

Power (Application of)

92 <u>Future Power</u>: <u>A Science Fiction Anthology</u>. Ed.
Jack Dann and Gardner Dozois. New York:
Random House, 1976. 256pp.

INTRODUCTION by Jack Dann and Gardner Dozois

THE DIARY OF THE ROSE by Ursula K. Le Guin
THE COUNTRY OF THE KIND by Damon Knight
SMOE AND THE IMPLICIT CLAY by R. A. Lafferty
SHE WAITS FOR ALL MEN BORN by James Tiptree, Jr.
THE DAY OF THE BIG TEST by Felix C. Gotschalk
CONTENTMENT, SATISFACTION, CHEER, WELL-BEING,
    GLADNESS, JOY, COMFORT, AND NOT HAVING TO GET
    UP EARLY ANY MORE by Geo. Alec Effinger
COMING-OF-AGE DAY by A. K. Jorgensson
THANATOS by Vonda N. McIntyre
THE EYEFLASH MIRACLES by Gene Wolfe

Prediction

The Professions

94   <u>Great Science Fiction About Doctors</u>. Ed. Groff
Conklin with Noah Fabricant, M.D. New York:
Collier Books, 1963. 412pp. [paper].

THE MAN WITHOUT AN APPETITE by Miles J. Breuer,
M.D.
OUT OF THE CRADLE, ENDLESSLY ORBITING by
Arthur C. Clarke
THE BROTHERS by Clifton L. Dance, Jr., M.D.
THE GREAT KEINPLATZ EXPERIMENT by Sir Arthur
Conan Doyle
COMPOUND B by David Harold Fink, M.D.
RAPPACCINI'S DAUGHTER by Nathaniel Hawthorne
THE PSYCHOPHONIC NURSE by David H. Keller, M.D.
THE LITTLE BLACK BAG by C. M. Kornbluth
RIBBON IN THE SKY by Murray Leinster
MATE IN TWO MOVES by Winston K. Marks
BEDSIDE MANNER by William Morrison
THE SHOPDROPPER by Alan Nelson
FAMILY RESEMBLANCE by Alan E. Nourse, M.D.
THE FACTS IN THE CASE OF M. VALDEMAR by Edgar
Allan Poe
EMERGENCY OPERATION by Arthur Porges
A MATTER OF ETHICS by J. R. Shango
BOLDEN'S PETS by F. L. Wallace
EXPEDITION MERCY by J. A. Winter, M.D.

Psychology

PREFACE by the Editors
INTRODUCTION: PSYCHOLOGY AND SCIENCE FICTION
   by the Editors

   1: PSYCHOBIOLOGY
SOCRATES by John Christopher
THE LYSENKO MAZE by Donald A. Wollheim
FLOWERS FOR ALGERNON by Daniel Keyes
NINE LIVES by Ursula K. Le Guin

   2: THE LEARNING PROCESS
THE MAN WHO DEVOURED BOOKS by John Sladek
LEARNING THEORY by James McConnell
SUSIE'S REALITY by Bob Stickgold

   3: SENSATION AND PERCEPTION
THE MAN IN THE RORSCHACH SHIRT by Ray Bradbury
SUCH STUFF by John Brunner
THE SUBLIMINAL MAN by J. G. Ballard
AND HE BUILT A CROOKED HOUSE by Robert A.
   Heinlein

   4: SOCIAL PROCESSES
ALL THE LAST WARS AT ONCE by Geo. Alec Effinger
LOVE, INCORPORATED by Robert Sheckley
SEVENTH VICTIM by Robert Sheckley
ADJUSTMENT by Ward Moore

Psychology

(Valence and Vision)

III. NATURE OR NURTURE—ONCE MORE WITH
      FEELING
VALENCE: GENETICS AND THE DIVERSITY OF BEHAVIOR
   by Theodosius Dobzhansky [essay]
VISION: PROFESSION by Isaac Asimov
VALENCE: A SCIENTIST'S VARIATIONS ON A DIS-
   TURBING RACIAL THEME by John Neary [essay]
VISION: LEARNING THEORY by James V. McConnell
VALENCE: THE CHEMISTRY OF LEARNING by David
   Krech [essay]

IV. THE EMERGENCY OF PARAPSYCHOLOGY
VALENCE: ESP AND CREDIBILITY IN SCIENCE by
   R. A. McConnell [essay]
VALENCE: PARAPSYCHOLOGY IN THE USSR by Stanley
   Kripper and Richard Davidson [essay]
VISION: FEAR HOUND by Katherine MacLean
VISION: MAD HOUSE by Richard Matheson

V. THE EXPLORATION AND CONTROL OF THE BRAIN
VALENCE: HOW THE MACHINE CALLED THE BRAIN FEELS
   AND THINKS by Dean E. Wooldridge [essay]
VISION: WILLIAM AND MARY by Roald Dahl
VALENCE: THE HAPPIEST CREATURES ON EARTH? by
   Ruth and Edward Brecher [essay]
VISION: PATENT PENDING by Arthur C. Clarke

VI. THE DISCOVERY OF ELBOW ROOM
VALENCE: O ROTTEN GOTHAM—SLIDING DOWN INTO THE
   BEHAVIORAL SINK by Tom Wolfe [essay]
VALENCE: BEHAVIORAL RESEARCH AND ENVIRONMENTAL
   PROGRAMMING by Robert Sommer [essay]
VISION: LIVING SPACE by Isaac Asimov

VII. A NEW LOOK AT THERAPY AND THE ASSESS-
      MENT OF PERSONALITY
VISION: Selection from BRAVE NEW WORLD by
   Aldous Huxley
VALENCE: ALL ABOUT THE NEW SEX THERAPY [essay]
VALENCE: THE SEX TESTERS [essay]

(Valence and Vision)
VISION: HE WHO SHAPES by Roger Zelazny
VALENCE: THERAPY IS THE HANDMAIDEN OF THE
   STATUS QUO by Seymour L. Halleck [essay]
VISION: THE MURDERER by Ray Bradbury
VISION: THE PETRIFIED WORLD by Robert Sheckley
   [essay]
VALENCE: THE MYTH OF THE MENTAL ILLNESS by
   Thomas Szasz

   VIII.   TESTING, MEASUREMENT, AND THE
      ULTIMATE EXPERIMENT
VALENCE: PSYCHOLOGICAL TESTING: A SMOKE SCREEN
   AGAINST LOGIC by Frank B. McMahon, Jr. [essay]
VISION: THE SIXTH PALACE by Robert Silverberg
VALENCE: WHAT CAN WE PREDICT? by Ruby Yoshioka
   [essay]
VISION: JOKESTER by Isaac Asimov

   IX.   WHO ARE THEY? WHO AM I—THE INCREASED
      RELEVANCY OF SOCIAL PSYCHOLOGY
VISION: THE DAY THE MARTIANS CAME by Frederik
   Pohl
VISION: SUNDANCE by Robert Silverberg
VALENCE: ARVN AS FAGGOTS: INVERTED WARFARE IN
   VIETNAM by Charles J. Levy [essay]
VISION: KNOTS by R. D. Laing

   X.   ON THE APPLICATION OF PSYCHOLOGY TO
      SOCIETY
VALENCE: SELECTIONS FROM BEYOND FREEDOM AND
   DIGNITY by B. F. Skinner [essay]
VISION: "REPENT HARLEQUIN!" SAID THE TICKTOCK-
   MAN by Harlan Ellison
VALENCE: THE PATHOS OF POWER by Kenneth Clark
   [essay]
VISION: THE FLYING MACHINE by Ray Bradbury

97   Introductory Psychology Through Science Fiction.
      2nd ed. Ed. Harvey A. Katz, Martin Harry Green-
      berg and Patricia S. Warrick. Chicago: Rand
      McNally, 1977. 550pp. [paper].

      INTRODUCTION: PSYCHOLOGY AND SCIENCE FICTION
        by the Editors

            1: DEVELOPMENTAL PROCESSES
      THAT ONLY A MOTHER by Judith Merril
      THE FIRST MEN by Howard Fast
      THE EXAMINATION by Felix Gotschalk
      THE PLAYGROUND by Ray Bradbury

            2: PSYCHOBIOLOGY
      FLOWERS FOR ALGERNON by Daniel Keyes
      THE BRAIN by Norbert Weiner
      SOCRATES by John Christopher
      NINE LIVES by Ursula K. Le Guin

            3: SENSATION, PERCEPTION, AND AWARENESS
      THROUGH OTHER EYES by R. A. Lafferty
      AND HE BUILT A CROOKED HOUSE by Robert A.
        Heinlein
      THE SUBLIMINAL MAN by J. G. Ballard
      SUCH STUFF by John Brunner

            4: LEARNING AND COGNITION
      LEARNING THEORY by James McConnell
      SUSIE'S REALITY by Bob Stickgold
      RAT IN THE SKULL by Rog Phillips
      THE MAN WHO DEVOURED BOOKS by John Sladek

            5: SOCIAL PROCESSES
      ALL THE LAST WARS AT ONCE by Geo. Alec Effinger
      ADJUSTMENT by Ward Moore
      SEVENTH VICTIM by Robert Sheckley
      LOVE, INCORPORATED by Robert Sheckley

            6: PERSONALITY
      MOTHER by Philip Jose Farmer
      DREAMING IS A PRIVATE THING by Isaac Asimov

Psychology

Religion

98   <u>Gods For Tomorrow</u>. Ed. Hans Stefan Santesson.
New York: Award Books, 1967. 208pp. [paper].

INTRODUCTION by Hans Stefan Santesson

THE STREETS OF ASHKELON by Harry Harrison
BALAAM by Anthony Boucher
UNHUMAN SACRIFICE by Katherine MacLean
THE SHRINE OF TEMPTATION by Judith Merril
THE ARMY COMES TO VENUS by Eric Frank Russell
APOSTLE TO ALPHA by Betty T. Balke
GOD OF THE PLAYBACK by Stephen Dentinger
ROBOT SON by Robert F. Young
THAT EVENING SUN GO DOWN by Arthur Sellings
THE WOLFRAM HUNTERS by Edward D. Hoch

99   <u>Other Worlds, Other Gods</u>: <u>Adventures in Religious
Science Fiction</u>. Ed. Mayo Mohs. Garden City:
Doubleday, 1971. 264pp.

INTRODUCTION: SCIENCE FICTION AND THE WORLD OF
RELIGION by Mayo Mohs

THE CUNNING OF THE BEAST by Nelson Bond
A CROSS OF CENTURIES by Henry Kuttner
SOUL MATE by Lee Sutton
THE WORD TO SPACE by Winston P. Sanders
PROMETHEUS by Philip Jose Farmer
THE NINE BILLION NAMES OF GOD by Arthur C.
   Clarke
THE VITANULS by John Brunner
JUDAS by John Brunner

(Other Worlds, Other Gods)
THE QUEST FOR SAINT AQUIN by Anthony Boucher
BALAAM by Anthony Boucher
EVENSONG by Lester del Rey
SHALL THE DUST PRAISE THEE? by Damon Knight
CHRISTUS APOLLO by Ray Bradbury

100   Signs and Wonders. Ed. Roger Elwood. Old Tappan,
      NJ: Fleming H. Revell, 1972. 157pp.

      INTRODUCTION by Roger Elwood

      MY FRIEND, KLATU by Laurence Yep
      TERRIBLE QUICK SWORD by Emil Petaja
      THE GENTLE CAPTIVE by Tom Godwin
      IN THE CUP by Barry N. Malzberg
      ALL IN GOOD TIME by Eando Binder
      A GLIMPSE OF MARY by Gordon A. Gyles
      THE IRON ONE by Edmond Hamilton
      TOWARDS THE BELOVED CITY by Philip Jose Farmer

101   Flame Tree Planet: An Anthology of Religious
      Science Fiction. Ed. Roger Elwood. St. Louis:
      Concordia, 1973. 159pp.

      INTRODUCTION: ROGER LOVIN

      FLAME TREE PLANET by George H. Smith
      POVERELLO by Raylyn Moore
      THE SINLESS CHILD by Dean R. Koontz
      APOSTLE by Roger Lovin
      A MATTER OF FREEDOMS by Clancy O'Brien
      HOW BRIGHT THE STARS by Leigh Brackett
      THE LIONS OF ROME by Raymond F. Jones
      MANY MANSIONS by Gail Kimberly
      BEARING WITNESS by Barry N. Malzberg
      TARRYING by Thomas N. Scortia

102   Chronicles of a Comer and Other Religious Science
      Fiction Stories. Ed. Roger Elwood. Atlanta:
      John Knox Press, 1974. 138pp. [paper].

(Chronicles of a Comer)

FOREWORD by Roger Elwood

THE PROBLEM OF PAIN by Poul Anderson
THE WOLFRAM HUNTERS by Edward D. Hoch
THE GIFT OF NOTHING by Joan C. Holly
TOWARDS THE BELOVED CITY by Philip Jose Farmer
CHRONICLES OF A COMER by K. M. O'Donnell
IN THIS SIGN by Ray Bradbury

CONTRIBUTORS

103   Strange Gods. Ed. Roger Elwood. New York:
      Pocket Books, 1974. 191pp. [paper].

      INTRODUCTION: WHATEVER GODS THERE BE: SPACE-
          TIME AND DEITY IN SCIENCE FICTION by George
          Zebrowski

      HIGH PRIEST by J. F. Bone
      OVERSIGHT by K. M. O'Donnell
      ONE AFTERNOON IN BUSTERVILLE by William K.
          Grasty
      THE PROPHET OF ZORAYNE by Terry Dixon
      IN HIS OWN IMAGE by Rachel Cosgrove Payes
      TRY AGAIN by Barry N. Malzberg
      CHOLOM by Virginia Kidd
      WHAT HATH GOD WROUGHT? by Lloyd Biggle, Jr.
      THROWBACK by Roger Elwood
      THE DIRECTOR by James Howard
      RETURN TO A HOSTILE PLANET by John B. Thomas
      MUSSPELSHEIM by Richard A. Lupoff

104   The New Awareness: Religion Through Science Fic-
      tion. Ed. Patricia Warrick and Martin Harry
      Greenberg. New York: Delacorte Press, 1975.
      485pp.

      PREFACE by the Editors
      INTRODUCTION by the Editors

Religion

(The New Awareness)

1: PRIMITIVE RELIGION
NIGHT OF THE LEOPARD by William Sambrot

2: THE POWER OF THE RELIGIOUS VISION
BEHOLD THE MAN by Michael Moorcock

3: RELIGIOUS INSTITUTIONS--PAST
A CANTICLE FOR LEIBOWITZ by Walter M. Miller,
Jr.

4: RELIGIOUS INSTITUTIONS--FUTURE
GOOD NEWS FROM THE VATICAN by Robert Silverberg

5: THE FALL FROM INNOCENCE
THE STREETS OF ASHKELON by Harry Harrison

6: THE NEED TO BELIEVE
ASK AND IT MAY BE GIVEN by Wesley Ford Davis

7: MORAL BEHAVIOR
THE COLD EQUATIONS by Tom Godwin

8: THE PROBLEM OF GOOD AND EVIL--A TAOISTIC
VIEW
DAZED by Theodore Sturgeon

9: BIRTH AND DEATH--MYTHS OF BEGINNING
EYES OF ONYX by Edward Bryant

10: THE APOCALYPTIC VISION OF THE END
THE NINE BILLION NAMES OF GOD by Arthur C.
Clarke

11: REGENERATION AND NEW BEGINNINGS
A ROSE FOR ECCLESIASTES by Roger Zelazny

12: THE PURPOSE OF MAN
EVOLUTION'S END by Robert Arthur

13: ALIEN INTELLIGENCE IN THE UNIVERSE
THE FIRE BALLOONS by Ray Bradbury

14: THE POWER OF LOVE
THE MAN WHO LEARNED LOVING by Theodore Sturgeon

Religion

The Sciences

MATHEMATICS AND PHILOSOPHY

Mathematics
WHAT DEAD MEN TELL by Theodore Sturgeon

Philosophy
REFERENT by Ray Bradbury

THE PHYSICAL SCIENCES

Geology and Geography
BLIND MAN'S BLUFF by Malcolm Jameson

Chemistry
PRESSURE by Ross Rocklynne

Physics
THE XI EFFECT by Philip Latham

Astronomy
OLD FAITHFUL by Raymond Z. Gallun

THE BIOLOGICAL SCIENCES

Biology
ALAS, ALL THINKING by Harry Bates

Bio-Chemistry
DUNE ROLLER by Julian C. May

Paleontology
EMPLOYMENT by L. Sprague de Camp

(Imagination Unlimited)

THE SOCIAL SCIENCES

Psychology
DREAMS ARE SACRED by Peter Phillips

Sociology
HOLD BACK TOMORROW by Kris Neville

Linguistics
BEROM by John Berryman

Anthropology
THE FIRE AND THE SWORD by Frank Robinson

106   Science in Fiction. Ed. A. E. and J. C. Bayliss.
      London: University of London, 1957. 191pp.

PRELUDE TO SPACE by Arthur C. Clarke [excerpt]
THE STAR by H. G. Wells
AN ANCIENT GULLIVER by Lucien [excerpt]
THE FLYING ISLAND by Jonathan Swift [excerpt]
A RACE WITH A DINOSAUR by Arthur Conan Doyle
   [excerpt]
AN EARLY TIME-TRAVELLER by Louis Sebastian
   Mercier [excerpt]
ADVENTURE IN A SPACE SHIP by C. S. Lewis
   [excerpt]
THE EXPERIMENTAL FARM by H. G. Wells [excerpt]
THE AVENGING RAY by Seamark [excerpt]
CAPTAIN NEMO'S THUNDERBOLT by Jules Verne
   [excerpt]
THE TRIFFID by John Wyndham [excerpt]
OFF OF THE MOON by Edwin F. Northrup [excerpt]

107   Fantasia Mathematica. Ed. Clifton Fadiman.
      New York: Simon and Schuster, 1958. 298pp.

INTRODUCTION by Clifton Fadiman

I.   Odd Numbers
YOUNG ARCHIMEDES by Aldous Huxley
PYTHAGORAS AND THE PSYCHOANALYST by Arthur
   Koestler

(Fantasia Mathematica)
  MOTHER AND THE DECIMAL POINT by Richard
    Llewellyn
  JURGEN PROVES IT BY MATHEMATICS by James Branch
    Cabell
  PETER LEARNS ARITHMETIC by H. G. Wells
  SOCRATES AND THE SLAVE by Plato
  THE DEATH OF ARCHIMEDES by Karel Capek

    II. Imaginaries
  THE DEVIL AND SIMON FLAGG by Arthur Porges
  -AND HE BUILT A CROOKED HOUSE by Robert A.
    Heinlein
  INFLEXIBLE LOGIC by Russell Maloney
  NO-SIDED PROFESSOR by Martin Gardner
  SUPERIORITY by Arthur C. Clarke
  THE MATHEMATICAL VOODOO by H. Nearing, Jr.
  EXPEDITION by Fredric Brown
  THE CAPTURED CROSS-SECTION by Miles J. Breuer,
    M.D.
  A. BOTTS AND THE MOEBIUS STRIP by William
    Hazlett Upson
  GOD AND THE MACHINE by Nigel Balchin
  THE TACHYPOMP by Edward Page Mitchell
  ISLAND OF FIVE COLORS by Martin Gardner
  THE LAST MAGICIAN by Bruce Elliot
  A SUBWAY NAMED MOEBIUS by A. J. Deutsch
  THE UNIVERSAL LIBRARY by Kurd Lasswitz
  POSTSCRIPT TO "THE UNIVERSAL LIBRARY" by Willy
    Ley
  JOHN JONES'S DOLLAR by Harry Stephen Keeler

  [The remaining sections of the table of contents
    have been omitted, as they comprise all non-
    fiction items.]

108   The Mathematical Magpie. Ed. Clifton Fadiman.
    New York: Simon & Schuster, 1962. 300pp.

    CARTOON by Abner Dean [drawing]
    INTRODUCTION by Clifton Fadiman

(The Mathematical Magpie)

    I. A Set of Imaginaries
CARTOON by Alan Dunn [drawing]
THE FEELING OF POWER by Isaac Asimov
THE LAW by Robert M. Coates
THE APPENDIX AND THE SPECTACLES by Miles J.
  Breuer, M.D.
PAUL BUNYON VERSUS THE CONVEYOR BELT by William
  Hazlett Upson
THE PACIFIST by Arthur C. Clarke
THE HERMENEUTICAL DOUGHNUT by N. Nearing, Jr.
STAR BRIGHT by Mark Clifton
FYI by James Blish
THE VANISHING MAN by Richard Hughes
THE NINE BILLION NAMES OF GOD by Arthur C.
  Clarke

[The remaining sections of the table of contents
have been omitted, as they comprise all non-
fiction items.]

109   Time Probe: The Sciences in Science Fiction. Ed.
    Arthur C. Clarke. New York: Delacorte Press,
    1966. 242pp.

INTRODUCTION: SCIENCE AND SCIENCE FICTION by
  Arthur C. Clarke

    Mathematics
--AND HE BUILT A CROOKED HOUSE by Robert A.
  Heinlein

    Cybernetics
THE WABBLER by Murray Leinster

    Meteorology
THE WEATHER MAN by Theodore L. Thomas

    Archaeology
THE ARTIFACT BUSINESS by Robert Silverberg

    Exobiology
GRANDPA by James H. Schmitz

(Time Probe)

    Physics
NOT FINAL! by Isaac Asimov

    Medicine
THE LITTLE BLACK BAG by Cyril Kornbluth

    Astronomy
THE BLINDNESS by Philip Latham

    Physiology
TAKE A DEEP BREATH by Arthur C. Clarke

    Chemistry
THE POTTERS OF FIRSK by Jack Vance

    Biology
THE TISSUE-CULTURE KING by Julian Huxley

110   Alchemy and Academe: A Collection of Original
Stories Concerning Themselves with Transmuta-
tions, Mental and Elemental, Alchemical and
Academic. Comp. Anne McCaffrey. New York:
Doubleday, 1970. 239pp.

FOREWORD by Anne McCaffrey

THE DANCE OF THE SOLIDS [poem] by John Updike
A MESS OF PORRIDGE by Sonya Dorman
THE INSTITUTE by Carol Emshwiller
CONDILLAC'S STATUE by R. A. Lafferty
THE SORCERERS [poem] by L. Sprague de Camp
THE WEED OF TIME by Norman Spinrad
NIGHT AND THE LOVES OF JOE DICOSTANZO by
    Samuel R. Delany
COME UP AND SEE ME by Daphne Castell
SHUT THE LAST DOOR by Joe Hensley
BIG SAM by Avram Davidson
MORE LIGHT by James Blish
THE MAN WHO COULD NOT SEE DEVILS by Joanna Russ
THE KEY TO OUT by Betsy Curtis
RINGING THE CHANGES by Robert Silverberg

(Alchemy and Academe)
   IN A QUART OF WATER by David Telfair
   MORNING-GLORY by Gene Wolfe
   ASCENSION: A WORKDAY ARABESQUE [poem] by
     Virginia Kidd
   THE DEVIL YOU DON'T by Keith Laumer
   THE TRIUMPHANT HEAD by Josephine Saxton
   MAINCHANCE by Peter Tate

111   Where Do We Go From Here? Ed. Isaac Asimov.
       Garden City: Doubleday, 1971. 441pp.

       INTRODUCTION by Isaac Asimov

       A MARTIAN ODYSSEY by Stanley G. Weinbaum
       NIGHT by Don A. Stuart
       THE DAY IS DONE by Lester del Rey
       HEAVY PLANET by Milton A. Rothman
       "--AND HE BUILT A CROOKED HOUSE--" by Robert A.
         Heinlein
       PROOF by Hal Clement
       A SUBWAY NAMED MOEBIUS by A. J. Deutsch
       SURFACE TENSION by James Blish
       COUNTRY DOCTOR by William Morrison
       THE HOLES AROUND MARS by Jerome Bixby
       THE DEEP RANGE by Arthur C. Clarke
       THE CAVE OF NIGHT by James E. Gunn
       DUST RAG by Hal Clement
       PATE DE FOIE GRAS by Isaac Asimov
       OMNILINGUAL by H. Beam Piper
       THE BIG BOUNCE by Walter S. Tevis
       NEUTRON STAR by Larry Niven

       APPENDIX

112   And Now Walk Gently Through the Fire. Ed. Roger
       Elwood. Philadelphia: Chilton, 1972. 176pp.
       [biochemistry].

       INTRODUCTION by Marsha Daly

       STELLA by Ted White
       MAKING IT THROUGH by Barry N. Malzberg

(And Now Walk Gently Through the Fire)
    AND NOW WALK GENTLY THROUGH THE FIRE by R. A.
      Lafferty
    THE GIFT OF NOTHING by Joan C. Holly
    FOREVER AND AMEN by Robert Bloch
    ...AND THE POWER by Rachel Cosgrove Payes
    CAUGHT IN THE ORGAN DRAFT by Robert Silverberg
    A SENSE OF DIFFERENCE by Pamela Sargent
    MOTHER EARTH WANTS YOU by Philip Jose Farmer
    CHRONICLES OF A COMER by K. M. O'Donnell

113   Bio-Futures: Science Fiction Stories about Bio-
       logical Metamorphosis. Ed. Pamela Sargent.
       New York: Vintage Books, 1976. 344pp. [paper].

    INTRODUCTION by Pamela Sargent

    THE PLANNERS by Kate Wilheim
    SLOW TUESDAY NIGHT by R. A. Lafferty
    IN RE GLOVER by Leonard Tushnet
    EMANCIPATION: A ROMANCE OF THE TIMES TO COME
      by Thomas M. Disch
    NINE LIVES by Ursula K. Le Guin
    CALL ME JOE by Poul Anderson
    THE IMMORTALS by James Gunn
    THE WEARIEST RIVER by Thomas N. Scortia
    DAY MILLION by Frederik Pohl
    WATERSHED by James Blish

    FURTHER READING

Sex

(Strange Bedfellows)

    PART TWO: TOUJOURS GAY
THE WORLD WELL LOST by Theodore Sturgeon
DO ANDROIDS DREAM OF ELECTRIC LOVE? by Walt
  Leibscher
DINNER AT HELEN'S by William Carlson

    PART THREE: YOU ONLY HURT THE ONE YOU LOVE
THE CRIMINAL by Joe Gores
THE MECHANICAL SWEETHEART by Gerald Arthur Alper
FALSE DAWN by Chelsea Quinn Yarbro
I'M WITH YOU IN ROCKLAND by Jack M. Dann

    PART FOUR: STRANGE MATINGS
DR. BIRDMOUSE by Reginald Bretnor
LOOKING—GLASS SEA by Laurence Yep
WHAT ABOUT US GRILS? by Mel Gilden

    PART FIVE: THE OLD—FASHIONED WAY?
LAMBETH BLOSSOM by Brian W. Aldiss
THE WIDENING CIRCLE by Richard McCloud
THE ICEBOX BLONDE by Thomas N. Scortia
KHARTOUM: A PROSE LIMERICK by Anthony Boucher

    PART SIX: A MOTHER'S LOVE
MOTHER by Philip Jose Farmer
THE DAUGHTER OF THE TREE by Miriam Allen deFord

116   Eros in Orbit: A Collection of All New Science
       Fiction Stories about Sex. Ed. Joseph Elder.
       New York: Trident Press, 1973. 189pp.

PREFACE by Joseph Elder

2.46593 by Edward Bryant
LOVEMAKER by Gordon Eklund
CLONE SISTER by Pamela Sargent
WHISTLER by Ron Goulart
IN THE GROUP by Robert Silverberg
FLOWERING NARCISSUS by Thomas N. Scortia
KIDDY—LIB by John Stopa

(Eros in Orbit)
DON SLOW AND HIS ELECTRIC GIRL GETTER by Thomas
  Brand
UPS AND DOWNS by Barry N. Malzberg
STARCROSSED by George Zebrowski

Sociology

Sociology

(The Sociology of the Possible)

conducting efficient elections
FRANCHISE by Isaac Asimov [excerpt]

from the secular to the sacred
A CANTICLE FOR LEIBOWITZ [novel] by Walter
Miller [excerpt]

III. FOUNDATIONS--social change

population, roles, and civilization
EARTH ABIDES [novel] by George Stewart [excerpt]

a tale of four cities
    a. suburbia
GLADIATOR-AT-LAW [novel] by Pohl and Kornbluth
[excerpt]

    b. a view from above
TORRENT OF FACES [novel] by Blish and Knight
[excerpt]

    c. a view from within
CAVES OF STEEL [novel] by Isaac Asimov [excerpt]

    d. a final solution
THE CITY AND THE STARS [novel] by Arthur C.
Clarke [excerpt]

technological innovation and social change
GADGET VERSUS TREND by Christopher Anvil

man versus machine: a conflict between
    species
EREHWON [novel] by Samuel Butler [excerpt]

a cybernated world
UTOPIA MINUS X [novel] by Rex Gordon [excerpt]

if all the world were like berkeley
WHAT TO DO TILL THE ANALYST COMES by Frederik
Pohl

(The Sociology of the Possible)

IV. WHOLES--social systems

the creation of a perfect society
THE REPUBLIC [non-fiction] by Plato [excerpt]

a utopian vision prior to the industrial
revolution
UTOPIA [novel] by Sir Thomas More [excerpt]

a utopia under conditions of affluence
LOOKING BACKWARDS [novel] by Edward Bellamy
[excerpt]

118 Above the Human Landscape: A Social Science Fiction Anthology. Ed. Willis E. McNelly and Leon
E. Stover. Pacific Palisades, CA: Goodyear,
1972. 387pp.

INTRODUCTION by Willis E. McNelly and Leon E.
Stover

Part one--Communities are for People
THE HIGHWAY by Ray Bradbury
THE WAVERIES by Fredric Brown
MOTHER OF NECESSITY by Chad Oliver
BLACK IS BEAUTIFUL by Robert Silverberg
GOLDEN ACRES by Kit Reed

Part two--Systems are for People
ADRIFT AT THE POLICY LEVEL by Chandler Davis
"REPENT, HARLEQUIN!" SAID THE TICKTOCKMAN by
Harlan Ellison
BALANCED ECOLOGY by James H. Schmitz
POSITIVE FEEDBACK by Christopher Anvil
POPPA NEEDS SHORTS by Walt and Leigh Richmond

Part three--Technology is for People
THE GREAT RADIO PERIL by Eric Frank Russell
RESCUE OPERATION by Harry Harrison
SLOW TUESDAY NIGHT by R. A. Lafferty
LIGHT OF OTHER DAYS by Bob Shaw
WHO CAN REPLACE A MAN? by Brian Aldiss

(Above the Human Landscape)

Part four--People Create Realities
WHAT WE HAVE HERE IS TOO MUCH COMMUNICATION by
Leon E. Stover
THE HANDLER by Damon Knight
THEY by Robert Heinlein
CARCINOMA ANGELS by Norman Spinrad
SHATTERED LIKE A GLASS GOBLIN by Harlan Ellison
THE NEW SOUND by Charles Beaumont

Part five--Tomorrow will be B(♀)tter
RAT RACE by Raymond F. Jones
COMING-OF-AGE DAY by A. K. Jorgensson
ECCE FEMINA! by Bruce McAllister
SEVENTH VICTIM by Robert Sheckley
ROOMMATES by Harry Harrison
MR. COSTELLO, HERO by Theodore Sturgeon

Afterword
SCIENCE FICTION AS CULTURE CRITICISM by the
Editors

PREFACE TO APPENDIX
Appendix 1
APEMAN, SUPERMAN--OR 2001'S ANSWER TO THE WORLD
RIDDLE by Leon E. Stover
Appendix 2
VONNEGUT'S SLAUGHTERHOUSE-FIVE: SCIENCE FICTION
AS OBJECTIVE CORRELATIVE by Willis E. McNelly

119   Sociology Through Science Fiction.   Ed. John W.
Milstead, Martin Harry Greenberg, Joseph D.
Olander and Patricia Warrick.   New York: St.
Martin's Press, 1974.   412pp.

INTRODUCTION by the Editors

1.   THE STUDY OF SOCIETY
LOST NEWTON by Stanley Schmidt
MISINFORMATION by Howard L. Myers

(Sociology Through Science Fiction)

    THE POLITICAL INSTITUTION
THE PEDESTRIAN by Ray Bradbury

    THE RELIGIOUS INSTITUTION
A CANTICLE FOR LEIBOWITZ by Walter M. Miller, Jr.

    6. POPULATION AND URBAN LIFE
TOTAL ENVIRONMENT by Brian W. Aldiss
SINGLE COMBAT by Robert Abernathy

120   Social Problems Through Science Fiction. Ed.
    Martin Harry Greenberg, John W. Milstead,
    Joseph D. Olander and Patricia Warrick. New
    York: St. Martin's Press, 1975. 356pp.

INTRODUCTION by the Editors

1. SOCIETY-WIDE PROBLEMS

    POPULATION PROBLEMS
THE PEOPLE TRAP by Robert Sheckley
THE SLICED-CROSSWISE ONLY-ON-TUESDAY WORLD by
   Philip Jose Farmer
BILLENIUM by J. G. Ballard

    RACE RELATIONS
THE NRACP by George P. Elliott
THE OTHER FOOT by Ray Bradbury

    ALIENATION AND URBAN SOCIETY
THE NUMBER YOU HAVE REACHED by Thomas M. Disch
THE VANISHING AMERICAN by Charles Beaumont

    DRUG USE AND DRUG ABUSE
NO DIRECTION HOME by Norman Spinrad

    SEXUAL DEVIANCE
THE WORLD WELL LOST by Theodore Sturgeon

2. PROBLEMS OF SOCIAL INSTITUTIONS

    THE FAMILY
THE FATHER-THING by Philip K. Dick
GOLDEN ACRES by Kit Reed

(Social Problems Through Science Fiction)

EDUCATION
THE GREAT INTELLECT BOOM by Christopher Anvil

ECONOMICS: WORK AND AUTOMATION
REVOLT OF THE POTATO-PICKER by Herb Lehrman

RELIGION
NIGHT OF THE LEOPARD by William Sambrot
GOOD NEWS FROM THE VATICAN by Robert Silverberg

POLITICAL INSTITUTIONS IN MASS SOCIETY
THE PRIZE OF PERIL by Robert Sheckley
ABOUT A SECRET CROCODILE by R. A. Lafferty

CRIME AND CRIMINAL JUSTICE
BOUNTY by T. L. Sherred
THE PUBLIC HATING by Steve Allen

SOCIAL SERVICES: POVERTY AND THE WELFARE
     SYSTEM
HOW I TAKE THEIR MEASURE by K. M. O'Donnell

SOCIAL SERVICE: MEDICAL CARE
A VISIT TO CLEVELAND GENERAL by Sydney Van Scyoc

121 Marriage and the Family Through Science Fiction.
     Ed. Val Clear, Patricia Warrick, Martin Harry
     Greenberg and Joseph D. Olander. New York:
     St. Martin's Press, 1976. 358pp.

INTRODUCTION by the Editors

     1. THE NATURE OF FAMILY ORGANIZATION
THE VINE by Kit Reed
TWENTY-FIRST CENTURY MOTHER by Katherine Marcuse
PILGRIMAGE by Nelson Bond
SPECIAL CONSENT by P. M. Hubbard

     2. CROSS-CULTURAL FAMILY PERSPECTIVES
THE ADJUSTED by Kenneth Bulmer

Sociology

<u>(Marriage and the Family Through Science Fiction)</u>

LOOK, YOU THINK YOU'VE GOT TROUBLES by Carol
  Carr
NO LAND OF NOD by Sherwood Springer

   3. THE SOCIOLOGY OF COURTSHIP
IN BEHALF OF THE PRODUCT by Kit Reed
LOVE, INCORPORATED by Robert Sheckley
THE COMPLEAT CONSUMATORS by Alan E. Nourse
EARTHWOMAN by R. Bretnor

   4. THE SOCIOLOGY OF MARRIAGE
THE GIRLS FROM EARTH by Frank M. Robinson
THE EDUCATION OF TIGRESS MCCARDLE by C. M.
  Kornbluth
PROGENY by Philip K. Dick
GIGOLO by Ron Goulart
CYNOSURE by Kit Reed
DAY MILLION by Frederik Pohl

   5. THE SOCIOLOGY OF FAMILY DISSOLUTION
THE ICEBOX BLONDE by Thomas N. Scortia
THE NEW YOU by Kit Reed
WOMAN'S RIB by Thomas N. Scortia
THE LAST LONELY MAN by John Brunner
THE LITTLE TERROR by Will F. Jenkins
FIRST LADY by J. T. McIntosh

   6. ALTERNATIVE FAMILY FORMS
THE REVOLT OF THE... by Robert Barr
WHEN IT CHANGED by Joanna Russ
CLONE SISTER by Pamela Sargent

The Solar System

(Great Science Fiction Stories about Mars)
>TIN LIZZIE by Randall Garrett
>UNDER THE SAND-SEAS by Oliver E. Saari
>OMNILINGUAL by H. Beam Piper

125   Great Science-Fiction Stories about the Moon.   Ed.
        T. E. Dikty.   New York: Frederick Fell, 1967.
        221pp.

        ACKNOWLEDGEMENTS
        INTRODUCTION: EARTH'S NATURAL SATELLITE by
          T. E. Dikty
        TABLE OF COMPARISONS: EARTH AND THE MOON by
          T. E. Dikty
        SIGNIFICANT EVENTS IN LUNAR EXPLORATION by
          T. E. Dikty

        MOON PROSPECTOR by William B. Ellern
        THE RELUCTANT HEROES by Frank M. Robinson
        GLIMPSES OF THE MOON by Wallace West
        THE PRO by Edmond Hamilton
        HONEYMOON IN HELL by Fredric Brown
        VIA DEATH by Eando Binder
        TRENDS by Isaac Asimov

        GLOSSARY [of space terms]

126   All about Venus: A Revelation of the Planet Venus
        in Fact and Fiction.   Ed. Brian W. Aldiss [with]
        Harry Harrison.   New York: Dell Books, 1968.
        219pp.   [paper].

        FOREWORD by Brian W. Aldiss

            I.   CLOUDED JUDGMENTS
        DESTINIES OF THE STARS by Svante Arrhenius
          [essay]
        LAST AND FIRST MEN [excerpt] by Olaf Stapledon
        PIRATES OF VENUS by Edgar Rice Burroughs
          [excerpt]
        PERELANDRA [excerpt] by C. S. Lewis

(All About Venus)

      II. "VENUS IS HELL"
EXPLORING THE PLANETS by V. A. Firsoff [excerpt, essay]
THE BIG RAIN by Poul Anderson
INTELLIGENT LIFE IN THE UNIVERSE by Carl Sagan [essay]

      III. BIG SISTER
ESCAPE TO VENUS by S. Markepeace Lott [excerpt]
SISTER PLANET by Poul Anderson
BEFORE EDEN by Arthur C. Clarke

      IV. THE OPEN QUESTION
SOME MYSTERIES OF VENUS RESOLVED by Sir Bernard Lovell [essay]
DREAM OF DISTANCE [anonymous fragment]
VENUS MYSTERY FOR SCIENTISTS by John Davy [essay]

BIBLIOGRAPHY OF PRINCIPAL NONFICTION WORKS CONSULTED

127   <u>Farewell, Fantastic Venus!</u> <u>A History of the Planet Venus in Fact and Fiction</u>. Ed. Brian W. Aldiss [with] Harry Harrison. London: Macdonald, 1968. 293pp.

ACKNOWLEDGMENTS
FOREWORD by Brian W. Aldiss

      SECTION I: CLOUDED JUDGMENTS
A TRIP TO VENUS by John Munro
THE STORY OF THE HEAVENS by Sir Robert Ball [essay]
HONEYMOON IN SPACE by George Griffith

      SECTION II: NEVER-FADING FLOWERS
THE DESTINIES OF THE STARS by Svante Arrhenius
LAST AND FIRST MEN by Olaf Stapledon [excerpt]
PIRATES OF VENUS by Edgar Rice Burroughs [excerpt]
PERELANDRA by C. S. Lewis [excerpt]

(Farewell, Fantastic Venus!)

SECTION III: SWAMP AND SAND
ALCHEMY by John and Dorothy de Courcy
THE MAN FROM VENUS by Frank R. Paul
A CITY ON VENUS by Henry Gade
UNVEILING THE MYSTERY PLANET by Willy Ley
   [essay]

SECTION IV: 'VENUS IS HELL!'
EXPLORING THE PLANETS by V. A. Firsoff [essay]
THE BIG RAIN by Poul Anderson
INTELLIGENT LIFE IN THE UNIVERSE by Carl Sagan
   [essay]

SECTION V: BIG SISTER
ESCAPE TO VENUS by S. Makepeace Lott
SISTER PLANET by Poul Anderson
BEFORE EDEN by Arthur C. Clarke

SECTION VI: THE OPEN QUESTION
SOME MYSTERIES OF VENUS RESOLVED by Sir Bernard
   Lovell [essay]
DREAM OF DISTANCE [anonymous essay]
VENUS MYSTERY FOR SCIENTISTS by John Davy
   [essay]

STOP PRESS:
SCIENTISTS SAY ICECAPS ON VENUS WOULD MAKE LIFE
   POSSIBLE [essay]

BIBLIOGRAPHY

128   Tomorrow's Worlds: Ten Stories of Science Fic-
      tion. Ed. Robert Silverberg. New York:
      Meredith Press, 1969. 234pp.

INTRODUCTION by Robert Silverberg

Mercury: SUNRISE ON MERCURY by Robert
               Silverberg
Venus: BEFORE EDEN by Arthur C. Clarke
Earth: SEEDS OF THE DUSK by Raymond Z.
               Gallun

(Tomorrow's Worlds)

Luna: THE BLACK PITS OF LUNA by Robert A. Heinlein

Mars: CRUCIFIXUS ETIAM by Walter M. Miller, Jr.

Jupiter: DESERTION by Clifford D. Simak

Saturn: PRESSURE by Harry Harrison

Uranus: THE PLANET OF DOUBT by Stanley G. Weinbaum

Neptune: ONE SUNDAY IN NEPTUNE by Alexei Panshin

Pluto: WAIT IT OUT by Larry Niven

129   First Flight To the Moon. Ed. Hal Clement. New York: Doubleday, 1970. 217pp.

FOREWORD by Hal Clement
INTRODUCTION by Isaac Asimov

   PART ONE: FICTION
EXTENDING THE HOLDINGS by David Grinnell
ONCE AROUND THE MOON by Vic Phillips
TRENDS by Isaac Asimov
THE MISSING SYMBOL by Paul W. Fairman
IDEAS DIE HARD by Isaac Asimov
JETSAM by A. Bertram Chandler
WRONG WAY STREET by Larry Niven
INTRUDERS by Edmund Cooper
REPORT ON THE NATURE OF THE LUNAR SURFACE by John Brunner
CRITICAL ANGLE by A. Bertram Chandler
VENTURE TO THE MOON by Arthur C. Clarke
MOONDUST, THE SMELL OF HAY, AND DIALECTICAL MATERIALISM by Thomas M. Disch

   PART TWO: HISTORY
[Omitted]

130 The Man in the Moon and Other Lunar Fantasies.
     Ed. Faith K. Pizor and Allan Comp. New York:
     Praeger Publishers, 1971. 230pp.

     LIST OF ILLUSTRATIONS
     REACHING FOR THE MOON: AN INTRODUCTION by
       Isaac Asimov

     From THE MAN IN THE MOON, OR A DISCOURSE OF A
       VOYAGE THITHER BY DOMINGO GONSALES THE SPEEDY
       MESSENGER (1638) by Francis Godwin
     From THE DISCOVERY OF A NEW WORLD,...WITH A DIS-
       COURSE CONCERNING THE POSSIBILITY OF A PASSAGE
       THITHER (1640) by John Wilkins
     From THE COMICAL HISTORY OF THE STATES AND EM-
       PIRES OF THE WORLD AND OF THE MOON (1656) by
       Cyrano de Bergerac
     From A VOYAGE TO CACKLOGALLINIA (1727) by
       "Captain Samuel Brunt"
     From THE LIFE AND ASTONISHING TRANSACTIONS OF
       JOHN DANIEL...(1751) by Ralph Morris
     A JOURNEY LATELY PERFORMED THROUGH THE AIR, IN
       AN AEROSTATIC GLOBE...TO THE NEWLY DISCOVERED
       PLANET, GEORGIUM SIDUS (1784) by "Vivenair"
     HANS PHAAL--A TALL TALE (1835) by Edgar Allan
       Poe
     From GREAT ASTRONOMICAL DISCOVERIES LATELY MADE
       BY SIR JOHN HERCHEL...AT THE CAPE OF GOOD
       HOPE (1835) by Richard Adams Locke
     THE GREAT STEAM-DUCK (1841) by "A Member of the
       L.L.B.B"

131 Mars, We Love You: Tales of Mars, Men, and Mar-
     tians. Ed. Jane Hipolito and Willis E. McNelly.
     Garden City: Doubleday, 1971. 332pp.

     FOREWORD by Jane Hipolito and Willis E. McNelly
     INTRODUCTION by Isaac Asimov

     REPORT ON CANALI by Giovanni Virginio
       Schiaparelli [non-fiction]

(Mars, We Love You)
    MARS AS THE ABODE OF LIFE by Percival Lowell
      [non-fiction]
    WAR OF THE WORLDS by H. G. Wells [excerpt]
    A PRINCESS OF MARS by Edgar Rice Burroughs
      [excerpt]
    A MARTIAN ODYSSEY by Stanley Weinbaum
    THE EMBASSY by Donald A. Wollheim
    DARK MISSION by Lester del Rey
    LOST ART by George O. Smith
    THE CAVE by P. Schuyler Miller
    EXPEDITION by Anthony Boucher
    LOOPHOLE by Arthur C. Clarke
    CATCH THAT MARTIAN by Damon Knight
    OMNILINGUAL by H. Beam Piper
    THE LOST CITY OF MARS by Ray Bradbury
    ONE STEP FROM EARTH by Harry Harrison
    CARTHAGE: REFLECTIONS OF A MARTIAN by Frank
      Herbert
    SOFT LANDING by William Fox
    EARTHBOUND by Irene Jackson
    IN LONELY LANDS by Harlan Ellison
    WORLD OF THE WARS by Bruce McAllister
    EXPLORATION by Barry N. Malzberg
    DOUBLE STAR by Robert A. Heinlein [excerpt]
    LINGUISTIC RELATIVITY IN MIDDLE HIGH MARTIAN
      by Willis E. McNelly [non-fiction]

132   <u>Jupiter</u>. Ed. Carol and Frederik Pohl. New York:
    Ballantine Books, 1973. 275pp. [paper].

    INTRODUCTION: JUPITER THE GIANT by Isaac Asimov
    PREFACE: JUPITER AT LAST by Frederik and Carol
      Pohl

    BRIDGE by James Blish
    VICTORY UNINTENTIONAL by Isaac Asimov
    DESERTION by Clifford D. Simak
    THE MAD MOON by Stanley G. Weinbaum
    HEAVYPLANET by Milton A. Rothman

(Jupiter)
  THE LOTUS-ENGINE by Raymond Z. Gallun
  CALL ME JOE by Poul Anderson
  HABIT by Lester del Rey
  A MEETING WITH MEDUSA by Arthur C. Clarke

Space Travel

133   Flight Into Space. Ed. Donald A. Wollheim. New
      York: Frederick Fell, 1950. 251pp.

      INTERPLANETARY TRAVEL SCIENCE FICTION
          STORIES
      SUNWARD by Stanton A. Coblentz
      THE MERCURIAN by Frank Belknap Long, Jr.
      PARASITE PLANET by Stanley G. Weinbaum
      PERIL OF THE BLUE WORLD by Robert Abernathy
      THE DEATH OF THE MOON by Alexander M. Phillips
      THE SEEKERS by Robert Moore Williams
      AJAX OF AJAX by Martin Pearson
      RED STORM ON JUPITER by Frank Belknap Long, Jr.
      HERMIT OF SATURN'S RING by Neil R. Jones
      PLANET PASSAGE by Donald A. Wollheim
      A BABY ON NEPTUNE by Clare Winger Harris and
          Miles J. Breuer, M.D.
      THE RAPE OF THE SOLAR SYSTEM by Leslie F. Stone

134   Men Against the Stars. Ed. Martin Greenberg.
      New York: Gnome Press, 1950. 351pp.

      FOREWORD by Martin Greenberg
      INTRODUCTION by Willy Ley

      TRENDS by Isaac Asimov
      MEN AGAINST THE STARS by Manly Wade Wellman
      THE RED DEATH OF MARS by Robert Moore Williams
      LOCKED OUT by H. B. Fyfe
      THE IRON STANDARD by Lewis Padgett
      SCHEDULE by Harry Walton
      FAR CENTAURUS by A. E. Van Vogt

(Men Against the Stars)
COLD FRONT by Hal Clement
THE PLANTS by Murray Leinster
COMPETITION by E. M. Hull
BRIDLE AND SADDLE by Isaac Asimov
WHEN SHADOWS FALL by L. Ron Hubbard

135   Possible Worlds of Science Fiction. Ed. Groff
       Conklin. New York: Vanguard Press, 1951.
       372pp.

           PART ONE: THE SOLAR SYSTEM
       OPERATION PUMICE by Raymond Z. Gallun
       THE BLACK PITS OF LUNA by Robert A. Heinlein
       ENCHANTED VILLAGE by A. E. Van Vogt
       LILIES OF LIFE by Malcolm Jameson
       ASLEEP IN ARMAGEDDON by Ray Bradbury
       NOT FINAL! by Isaac Asimov
       CONES by Frank Belknap Long, Jr.
       MOON OF DELIRIUM by D. L. James
       COMPLETELY AUTOMATIC by Theodore Sturgeon
       THE DAY WE CELEBRATE by Nelson Bond
       THE PILLOWS by Margaret St. Clair
       PROOF by Hal Clement

           PART TWO: THE GALAXY
       PROPAGANDIST by Murray Leinster
       IN VALUE DECEIVED by H. B. Fyfe
       HARD LUCK DIGGINGS by Jack Vance
       SPACE RATING by John Berryman
       CONTAGION by Katherine MacLean
       LIMITING FACTOR by Clifford D. Simak
       EXIT LINE by Sam Merwin, Jr.
       SECOND NIGHT OF SUMMER by James H. Schmitz
       A WALK IN THE SUN by Arthur C. Clarke
       THE HELPING HAND by Poul Anderson

136   Travelers of Space. Ed. Martin Greenberg. New
       York: Gnome Press, 1952. 400pp.

(Travelers of Space)

ARTICLES

PREFACE TO SCIENCE FICTION DICTIONARY by Samuel
Anthony Peeples

SCIENCE FICTION DICTIONARY

FICTION

THE ROCKETEERS HAVE SHAGGY EARS by Keith
Bennett

CHRISTMAS TREE by Christopher S. Youd

THE FORGIVENESS OF TENCHU TAEN by F. A. Kummer,
Jr.

EPISODE ON DHEE MINOR by Harry Walton

THE SHAPE OF THINGS by Ray Bradbury

COLUMBUS WAS A DOPE by Lyle Monroe

ATTITUDE by Hal Clement

THE IONIAN CYCLE by William Tenn

TROUBLE ON TANTALUS by P. Schuyler Miller

PLACET IS A CRAZY PLACE by Fredric Brown

ACTION ON AZURA by Robertson Osborne

THE RULL by A. E. Van Vogt

THE DOUBLE-DYED VILLAINS by Poul Anderson

BUREAU OF SLICK TRICKS by H. B. Fyfe

137   Space Service. Ed. Andre Norton. Cleveland:
World, 1953. 277pp.

COMMAND by Bernard I. Kahn

STAR-LINKED by H. B. Fyfe

CHORE FOR A SPACEMAN by Walt Sheldon

THE SPECTER GENERAL by Theodore R. Cogswell

IMPLODE AND PEDDLE by H. B. Fyfe

STEEL BROTHER by Gordon R. Dickson

FOR THE PUBLIC by Bernard I. Kahn

EXPEDITION POLYCHROME by J. A. Winter, M.D.

RETURN OF A LEGEND by Raymond Z. Gallun

THAT SHARE OF GLORY by C. M. Kornbluth

138   Space Pioneers. Ed. Andre Norton. Cleveland:
World, 1954. 294pp.

THE EXPLORERS

Earth
THE ILLUSIONARIES by Eric Frank Russell

Moon
MOONWALK by H. B. Fyfe

Mars
TRAIL BLAZER by Raymond Z. Gallun

Other Systems
THOU GOOD AND FAITHFUL by K. Houston Brunner

THE SETTLERS

Earth
A PAIL OF AIR by Fritz Leiber

Mars
THE FARTHEST HORIZON by Raymond F. Jones

Asteroid Belt
ASTEROID OF FEAR by Raymond Z. Gallun

Other Systems
PAGE AND PLAYER by Jerome Bixby

139   Tales of Outer Space. Ed. Donald A. Wollheim.
New York: Ace Books, 1954. 140pp. [paper].

TO THE MOON
DOORWAY IN THE SKY by Ralph Williams

TO MARS
HERE LIE WE by Fox B. Holden

TO THE SUN'S EDGE
OPERATION MERCURY by Clifford D. Simak

TO THE STARS
LORD OF A THOUSAND SUNS by Poul Anderson

(Tales of Outer Space)
BEYOND THE STARS
BEHIND THE BLACK NEBULA by L. Ron Hubbard

140   Adventures On Other Planets. Ed. Donald A. Woll-
       heim. New York: Ace Books, 1955. 160pp.
       [paper].

       ON VENUS
       THE OBLIGATION by Roger Dee

       ON MARS
       THE SOUND OF BUGLES by Robert Moore Williams

       ON A PLANET OF SIGMA DRACONIS
       OGRE by Clifford D. Simak

       ON A WORLD IN THE "BORNIK" STAR CLUSTER
       ASSIGNMENT ON PASIK by Murray Leinster

       ON LAERTES III
       THE RULL by A. E. Van Vogt

141   Exploring Other Worlds. Ed. Sam Moskowitz. New
       York: Collier Books, 1963. 256pp. [paper].

       THE MAD MOON by Stanley G. Weinbaum
       GARDEN IN THE VOID by Poul Anderson
       AT THE CENTER OF GRAVITY by Ross Rocklynne
       SOMETHING GREEN by Fredric Brown
       THE DEAD PLANET by Edmond Hamilton
       THE RADIANT ENEMIES by R. F. Starzl
       VIA ASTEROID by Eando Binder
       MAN OF THE STARS by Sam Moskowitz

142   First Flight: Maiden Voyages In Space and Time.
       Ed. Damon Knight. New York: Lancer Books,
       1963. 160pp. [paper].

       THE ISOLINGUALS by L. Sprague de Camp
       THE FAITHFUL by Lester del Ray
       BLACK DESTROYER by A. E. Van Vogt

(First Flight)
LIFE-LINE by Robert A. Heinlein
ETHER BREATHER by Theodore Sturgeon
LOOPHOLE by Arthur C. Clarke
TOMORROW'S CHILDREN by Poul Anderson
THAT ONLY A MOTHER by Judith Merril
WALK TO THE WORLD by Algis Budrys
T by Brian W. Aldiss

143   Great Stories of Space Travel. Ed. Groff Conklin.
       New York: Tempo Books, 1963. 256pp. [paper].

       INTRODUCTION by Groff Conklin

            THE SOLAR SYSTEM...
       THE WINGS OF NIGHT by Lester del Rey
       THE HOLES AROUND MARS by Jerome Bixby
       KALEIDOSCOPE by Ray Bradbury
       I'LL BUILD YOUR DREAM CASTLE by Jack Vance

            ...AND BEYOND THE SOLAR SYSTEM
       FAR CENTAURUS by A. E. Van Vogt
       PROPAGANDIST by Murray Leinster
       CABIN BOY by Damon Knight
       A WALK IN THE DARK by Arthur C. Clarke
       BLIND ALLEY by Isaac Asimov
       THE HELPING HAND by Poul Anderson
       ALLAMAGOOSA by Eric Frank Russell

144   More Adventures On Other Planets. Ed. Donald A.
       Wollheim. New York: Ace Books, 1963. 190pp.
       [paper].

       CHILD OF THE SUN by Leigh Brackett
       SUNRISE ON MERCURY by Robert Silverberg
       BY THE NAME OF MAN by John Brunner
       THE RED DEATH OF MARS by Robert Moore Williams
       THE PLANET OF DOUBT by Stanley G. Weinbaum
       TIGER BY THE TAIL by Poul Anderson

145   <u>Another Part of the Galaxy</u>. Ed. Groff Conklin.
        Greenwich, CT: Fawcett Gold Medal, 1966.
        224pp. [paper].

        INTRODUCTION by Groff Conklin

        THE RED HILLS OF SUMMER by Edgar Pangborn
        BIG SWORD by Paul Ash
        FIRST LADY by J. T. McIntosh
        INSIDEKICK by J. F. Bone
        THE LIVE COWARD by Poul Anderson
        STILL LIFE by Eric Frank Russell

146   <u>The Farthest Reaches</u>. Ed. Joseph Elder.
        New York: Trident Press, 1968. 217pp.

        FOREWORD by Joseph Elder

        THE WORM THAT FLIES by Brian W. Aldiss
        KYRIE by Poul Anderson
        TOMORROW IS A MILLION YEARS by J. G. Ballard
        POND WATER by John Brunner
        THE DANCE OF THE CHANGER AND THE THREE by
          Terry Carr
        CRUSADE by Arthur C. Clarke
        RANGING by John Jakes
        MIND OUT OF TIME by Keith Laumer
        THE INSPECTOR by James McKimmey
        TO THE DARK STAR by Robert Silverberg
        A NIGHT IN ELF HILL by Norman Spinrad
        SULWEN'S PLANET by Jack Vance

147   <u>First Step Outward</u>. Ed. Robert Hoskins. New
        York: Dell Books, 1967. 224pp. [paper].

        INTRODUCTION by Poul Anderson
        PROLOGUE by Robert Hoskins

           TO SPACE
        COLD WAR by Kris Neville
        THIRD STAGE by Poul Anderson
        GENTLEMEN, BE SEATED by Robert A. Heinlein
        JAYWALKER by Ross Rocklynne

(First Step Outward)

    TO THE PLANETS
THE HATED by Frederik Pohl
SUNRISE ON MERCURY by Robert Silverberg
HOP-FRIEND by Terry Carr
THE MAN WHO LOST THE SEA by Theodore Sturgeon

    TO THE STARS
FIRST CONTACT by Murray Leinster
MISBEGOTTEN MISSIONARY by Isaac Asimov
THE MARKET IN ALIENS by K. M. O'Donnell
THE RULES OF THE ROAD by Norman Spinrad

    EPILOG
JETSAM by A. Bertram Chandler

148   To the Stars: Eight Stories of Science Fiction.
    Ed. Robert Silverberg. New York: Hawthorn
    Books, 1971. 255pp.

ACKNOWLEDGMENTS
INTRODUCTION by Robert Silverberg

COMMON TIME by James Blish
FOUR IN ONE by Damon Knight
OZYMANDIAS by Robert Silverberg
THE END OF THE LINE by James H. Schmitz
A WALK IN THE DARK by Arthur C. Clarke
PLANETOID IDIOT by Phyllis Gotleib
THE KEYS TO DECEMBER by Roger Zelazny
GYPSY by Poul Anderson

149   Worlds Apart. Ed. George Locke. London:
    Cornmarket Reprints, 1972. 180pp.

INTRODUCTION by George Locke

LETTERS FROM THE PLANETS by W. S. Lach-Szyrma
    A RUINED CITY IN THE MOON
    IN THE ANTARCTIC REGIONS OF MARS
    THE QUEEN OF BEAUTY, OR THE PLANET OF LOVE
    MERCURY

(Worlds Apart)
    THE PORTALS OF THE KING OF DAY
    OUR SECOND VOYAGE TO MARS
    CANAL LIFE ON MARS
    A TRIP TO JUPITER'S MOONLET
    CORRESPONDING WITH THE PLANETS
THE REJECTED PLANET by John Fleming Wilson
THE GREAT SACRIFICE by George C. Wallis
IN THE DEEP OF TIME by George Parsons
THE STRANGE CASE OF ALAN MORAINE by Bertram
  Atkey
THE WHEELS OF DR. GINOCHIO GYVES by Ellsworth
  Douglass and Edwin Pallander
A MESSAGE FROM THE MOON by George Allan England
THE BLACK SHADOW by Owen Oliver
STORIES OF OTHER WORLDS by George Griffith
    A VISIT TO THE MOON
    THE WORLD OF THE WAR GOD
    A GLIMPSE OF THE SINLESS STAR
    THE WORLD OF CRYSTAL CITIES
    IN SATURN'S REALM
    HOMEWARD BOUND

150   Deep Space: Eight Stories of Science Fiction.
    Ed. Robert Silverberg. Nashville: Thomas
    Nelson, 1973. 183pp.

INTRODUCTION by Robert Silverberg

BLOOD'S A ROVER by Chad Oliver
NOISE by Jack Vance
LIFE HUTCH by Harlan Ellison
TICKET TO ANYWHERE by Damon Knight
THE SIXTH PALACE by Robert Silverberg
LULUNGOMEENA by Gordon R. Dickson
THE DANCE OF THE CHANGER AND THE THREE by Terry
  Carr
FAR CENTAURUS by A. E. Van Vogt

151   Explorers of Space: Eight Stories of Science
       Fiction. Ed. Robert Silverberg. Nashville:
       Thomas Nelson, 1975. 253pp.

       INTRODUCTION by Robert Silverberg

       EXPLORATION TEAM by Murray Leinster
       BEACHHEAD by Clifford D. Simak
       KYRIE by Poul Anderson
       JUPITER FIVE by Arthur C. Clarke
       COLLECTING TEAM by Robert Silverberg
       EACH AN EXPLORER by Isaac Asimov
       VASTER THAN EMPIRES, AND MORE SLOW by Ursula K.
          Le Guin
       WHAT'S IT LIKE OUT THERE? by Edmond Hamilton

152   Faster Than Light: An Original Anthology about
       Interstellar Travel. Ed. Jack Dann and George
       Zebrowski. New York: Harper & Row, 1976.
       321pp.

       INTRODUCTION: DREAMING AGAIN by Jack Dann and
          George Zebrowski

       THE ULTIMATE SPEED LIMIT by Isaac Asimov [essay]
       POSSIBLE, THAT'S ALL! by Arthur C. Clarke
          [essay]
       THE LIMITING VELOCITY OF ORTHODOXY by Keith
          Laumer [essay]
       BUT WHAT IF WE TRIED IT? by Ben Bova [essay]
       SUN UP by A. A. Jackson IV and Howard Waldrop
       DIALOGUE by Poul Anderson
       LONGLINE by Hal Clement
       PHOENIX WITHOUT ASHES by Harlan Ellison
       THE EVENT HORIZON by Ian Watson
       NOR THE MANY-COLORED FIRES OF A STAR RING by
          George R. R. Martin
       DEAD IN IRONS by Chelsea Quinn Yarbro
       SEASCAPE by Gregory Benford
       FAST-FRIEND by George R. R. Martin
       HYPERSPACE by Dick Allen [poem]

(<u>Faster Than Light</u>)

Sports

INTRODUCTION by the Editors

    FOOTBALL
THE LAST SUPER BOWL GAME by George R. R. Martin
THE NATIONAL PASTIME by Norman Spinrad
RUN TO STARLIGHT by George R. R. Martin

    BASEBALL
DODGER FAN by Will Stanton
THE CELEBRATED NO-HIT INNING by Frederik Pohl
NAKED TO THE INVISIBLE EYE by George Alec
  Effinger

    BASKETBALL
GOAL TENDING by E. Michael Blake

    GOLF
TO HELL WITH THE ODDS by Robert L. Fish

    BOXING
TITLE FIGHT by William Campbell Gault
STEEL by Richard Matheson

    CHESS
THE IMMORTAL GAME by Poul Anderson

    FISHING
THE DOORS OF HIS FACE, THE LAMPS OF HIS MOUTH
  by Roger Zelazny

(Run to Starlight)

    HUNTING
    POOR LITTLE WARRIOR! by Brian W. Aldiss

154   Arena: Sports SF. Ed. Edward L. Ferman and
    Barry N. Malzberg. New York: Doubleday, 1976.
    223pp.

    INTRODUCTION by Edward L. Ferman

    WHISPERS IN BEDLAM by Irwin Shaw
    MIRROR OF ICE by Gary Wright
    DODGER FAN by Will Stanton
    CLOSED SICILIAN by Barry N. Malzberg
    ARENA by Fredric Brown
    NOBODY BOTHERS GUS by Algis Budrys
    OPEN WARFARE by James E. Gunn
    GLADYS'S GREGORY by John Anthony West
    THE NIGHT BOXING ENDED by Bruce Jay Friedman
    BEYOND THE GAME by Vance Aandahl
    THE HUNGARIAN CINCH by Bill Pronzini

    AFTERWORD: ON THE NON-TRANSCENDENCE OF SPORT
      by Barry N. Malzberg

155   The Infinite Arena: Seven Science Fiction Stories
    about Sports. Ed. Terry Carr. Nashville:
    Thomas Nelson, 1977. 191pp.

    INTRODUCTION by Terry Carr

    JOY IN MUDVILLE by Poul Anderson and Gordon R.
      Dickson
    BULLARD REFLECTS by Malcolm Jameson
    THE BODY BUILDERS by Keith Laumer
    THE GREAT KLADNAR RACE by Robert Silverberg and
      Randall Garrett
    MR. MEEK PLAYS POLO by Clifford D. Simak
    SUNJAMMER by Arthur C. Clarke
    RUN TO STARLIGHT by George R. R. Martin

Superior Powers

(14 Great Tales of ESP)
I'M A STRANGER HERE MYSELF by Mack Reynolds
THE MAN ON TOP by R. Bretnor
FALSE IMAGE by Jay Williams
ARARAT by Zenna Henderson
THESE ARE THE ARTS by James H. Schmitz
THE GARDEN IN THE FOREST by Robert F. Young
AND STILL IT MOVES by Eric Frank Russell [essay]

158   Mind to Mind: Nine Stories of Science Fiction.
       Ed. Robert Silverberg. Nashville: Thomas
       Nelson, 1971. 270pp.

       INTRODUCTION by Robert Silverberg

       THE MINDWORM by C. M. Kornbluth
       PSYCLOPS by Brian W. Aldiss
       NOVICE by James H. Schmitz
       LIAR! by Isaac Asimov
       SOMETHING WILD IS LOOSE by Robert Silverberg
       RIYA'S FOUNDLING by Algis Budrys
       THROUGH OTHER EYES by R. A. Lafferty
       THE CONSPIRATORS by James White
       JOURNEYS END by Poul Anderson

159   Young Demons. Ed. Roger Elwood and Vic Ghidalia.
       New York: Avon Books, 1972. 160pp. [paper].

       INTRODUCTION by Theodore Sturgeon

       SREDNI VASHTAR by Saki (H. H. Munro)
       BETTYANN by Kris Neville
       THE TRANSCENDENT TIGERS by R. A. Lafferty
       APPLE by Anne McCaffrey
       THE SMALL ASSASSIN by Ray Bradbury
       SHUT THE LAST DOOR by Joe Hensley
       GAMES by Katherine MacLean
       JAMBOREE by Jack Williamson

160   Demon Kind. Ed. Roger Elwood. New York: Avon
       Books, 1973. 192pp. [paper].

(Demon Kind)

INTRODUCTION by Roger Elwood

LINKAGE by Barry Malzberg
MUD VIOLET by R. A. Lafferty
BETTYANN'S CHILDREN by Kris Neville
CHILD by Joan C. Holly
WORLD OF GRAY by Norman Spinrad
DANDY by Ted White
A PROPER SANTA CLAUS by Anne McCaffrey
THE MARKS OF PAINTED TEETH by Jack Dann
THE EDDYSTONE LIGHT by Laurence Yep
FROM DARKNESS TO DARKNESS by Terry Carr
MONOLOGUE by Philip Jose Farmer

161   Frontiers 2: The New Mind. Ed. Roger Elwood.
        New York and London: Macmillan, 1973. 180pp.

PREFACE by Roger Elwood
INTRODUCTION by Frederik Pohl

THE MAGIC CHILD by C. L. Grant
VACATION by Richard Posner
FOUR SIDES OF INFINITY by R. A. Lafferty
FROM ALL OF US by Gerard M. Bauer
NEW NEW YORK NEW ORLEANS by Geo. Alec Effinger
I AM ALEPPO by Jerry Sohl
OPENING FIRE by Barry N. Malzberg
SPACE TO MOVE by Joseph Green
BRAIN WIPE by Katherine MacLean

162   The Oddballs. Ed. Vic Ghidalia. New York:
        Manor Books, 1973. 190pp. [paper].

THE MAN WHO COULD WORK MIRACLES by H. G. Wells
THE LUNATIC PLANET by Robert Silverberg
NOBODY BOTHERS GUS by Algis Budrys
THE DREAMS OF ALBERT MORELAND by Fritz Leiber
THE MAN WHO WALKED THROUGH GLASS by Nelson Bond
TALENT by Robert Bloch

(The Oddballs)
THE BARBARIAN by Poul Anderson
EACH AN EXPLORER by Isaac Asimov
PASSING OF THE THIRD FLOOR BACK by Jerome K.
   Jerome

163   Strange Gifts: Eight Stories of Science Fiction.
      Ed. Robert Silverberg. Nashville: Thomas
      Nelson, 1975.   191pp.

      INTRODUCTION by Robert Silverberg

      THE GOLDEN MAN by Philip K. Dick
      DANGER-HUMAN! by Gordon R. Dickson
      ALL THE PEOPLE by R. A. Lafferty
      ODDY AND ID by Alfred Bester
      THE MAN WITH ENGLISH by Horace L. Gold
      TO BE CONTINUED by Robert Silverberg
      HUMPTY DUMPTY HAD A GREAT FALL by Frank Belknap
         Long
      BETTYANN by Kris Neville

Time

Time

Time Travel

THROUGH THE CLOCK
THE TIME MACHINE by H. G. Wells
ELSEWHERE AND OTHERWISE by Algernon Blackwood
ENOCH SOAMES by Max Beerbohm
BETWEEN THE MINUTE AND THE HOUR by A. M. Burrage

THE SHAPE OF THINGS TO COME
THE ROCKING-HORSE WINNER by D. H. Lawrence
ON THE STAIRCASE by Katherine Fullerton Gerould
AUGUST by W. F. Harvey
THE ANTICIPATOR by Morley Roberts
THE OLD MAN by Holloway Horn
THE TAIPAN by W. Somerset Maugham
THE HOUSING OF MR. BRADEGAR by H. F. Heard

THE PAST REVISITED
"THE FINEST STORY IN THE WORLD" by Rudyard
  Kipling
ETCHED IN MOONLIGHT by James Stephens
A VIEW FROM A HILL by M. R. James
A FRIEND TO ALEXANDER by James Thurber
THE SILVER MIRROR by A. Conan Doyle

WHEN TIME STOOD STILL
NO SHIPS PASS by Lady Eleanor Smith
THE CLOCK by A. E. W. Mason
OPENING THE DOOR by Arthur Machen

(Travelers In Time)

    TIME OUT OF JOINT
THE CURIOUS CASE OF BENJAMIN BUTTON by F. Scott
  Fitzgerald
THE ALTERNATIVE by Maurice Baring

    VISITORS FROM OUT OF TIME
MR. STRENBERRY'S TALE by J. B. Priestly
PHANTAS by Oliver Onions
THE HOMELESS ONE by A. E. Coppard

167   <u>Voyagers In Time</u>: <u>Twelve Stories of Science Fic-
    tion</u>. Ed. Robert Silverberg. New York:
    Hawthorn Books, 1967. 243pp.

    INTRODUCTION by Robert Silverberg

    THE SANDS OF TIME by P. Schuyler Miller
    ...AND IT COMES OUT HERE by Lester del Rey
    BROOKLYN PROJECT by William Tenn
    THE MEN WHO MURDERED MOHAMMED by Alfred Bester
    TIME HEALS by Poul Anderson
    WRONG-WAY STREET by Larry Niven
    FLUX by Michael Moorcock
    DOMINOES by C. M. Kornbluth
    A BULLETIN FROM THE TRUSTEES by Wilma Shore
    TRAVELER'S REST by David I. Masson
    ABSOLUTELY INFLEXIBLE by Robert Silverberg
    THE TIME MACHINE [Chapter XI, XII-part] by
      H. G. Wells

168   <u>Elsewhere and Elsewhen</u>. Ed. Groff Conklin.
    New York: Berkeley Medallion, 1968. 253pp.
    [paper].

    INTRODUCTION by Groff Conklin

      ELSEWHEN
    SHORTSTACK by Walt and Leigh Richmond
    HOW ALLIED by Mark Clifton
    THE WRONG END by J. T. McIntosh
    WORLD IN A BOTTLE by Allen Kim Lang

(Elsewhere and Elsewhen)

 ELSEWHERE
THINK BLUE, COUNT TWO by Cordwainer Smith
TURNING POINT by Poul Anderson
THE BOOK by Michael Shaara
TROUBLE TIDE by James H. Schmitz
THE EARTHMAN'S BURDEN by Donald E. Westlake

169 The Time Curve. Ed. Sam Moskowitz and Roger
   Elwood. New York: Tower Books, 1968. 189pp.
   [paper].

  UNTO HIM THAT HATH by Lester del Rey
  NICE GIRL WITH 5 HUSBANDS by Fritz Leiber
  DEATH OF A DINOSAUR by Sam Moskowitz
  TERROR OUT OF TIME by Jack Williamson
  TIME WOUNDS ALL HEELS by Robert Bloch
  OVER THE RIVER AND THROUGH THE WOODS by
   Clifford D. Simak
  A GUN FOR DINOSAUR by L. Sprague de Camp
  OPERATION PEEP by John Wyndham

   BONUS SECTION
  THE GREAT JUDGE by A. E. Van Vogt
  THE GIFTS OF ASTI by Andre Norton

170 Strange Adventures in Time. Ed. Roger Lancelyn
   Green. London: J. M. Dent, 1974. 147pp.

  INTRODUCTION by Roger Lancelyn Green

  RIP VAN WINKLE by Washington Irving
  THE FINEST STORY IN THE WORLD by Rudyard Kipling
  THE MYSTERY OF JOSEPH LAQUEDEM by Sir Arthur
   Quiller-Couch
  THE MAN WHO COULD WORK MIRACLES by H. G. Wells
  THE LEFT-HANDED SWORD by E. Nesbit
  THE SILVER MIRROR by Sir Arthur Conan Doyle
  SPACE by John Buchan
  THE CRYSTAL TRENCH by A. E. W. Mason
  THREE GHOSTS by John Keir Cross

171   <u>Trips in Time</u>: <u>Nine Stories of Science Fiction</u>.
      Ed. Robert Silverberg. Nashville: Thomas
      Nelson, 1977. 174pp.

      INTRODUCTION by Robert Silverberg

      AN INFINITE SUMMER by Christopher Priest
      THE KING'S WISHES by Robert Sheckley
      MANNA by Peter Phillips
      THE LONG REMEMBERING by Poul Anderson
      TRY AND CHANGE THE PAST by Fritz Leiber
      DIVINE MADNESS by Roger Zelazny
      MUGWUMP 4 by Robert Silverberg
      SECRET RIDER by Martha Randall
      THE SEESAW by A. E. Van Vogt

Utopia

BUCK ROGERS IN THE NEW JERUSALEM: INTRODUCTION
  by Thomas M. Disch

HEAVENS BELOW: FIFTEEN UTOPIAS by John Sladek
REPAIRING THE OFFICE by Charles Naylor
WHAT YOU GET FOR YOUR DOLLAR by Brian W. Aldiss
THE PEOPLE OF PRASHAD by James Keilty
A FEW THINGS I KNOW ABOUT WHILEAWAY by Joanna
  Russ
DRUMBLE by Cassandra Nye
A CLEAR DAY IN THE MOTOR CITY by Eleanor Arnason
SETTLING THE WORLD by M. John Harrison
I ALWAYS DO WHAT TEDDY SAYS by Harry Harrison
PYRAMIDS FOR MINNESOTA: A SERIOUS PROPOSAL by
  Thomas M. Disch
THE ZEN ARCHER by Jonathan Greenblatt
THE HERO AS WEREWOLF by Gene Wolfe

War

173 The War Book. Ed. James Sallis. London: Rupert Hart-Davis, 1969. 188pp.

INTRODUCTION by James Sallis

THE PRICE by Algis Budrys
IN PASSAGE OF THE SUN by George Collyn
1-A by Thomas M. Disch
GAME by Donald Barthelme
THE FOXHOLES OF MARS by Fritz Leiber
DOWN THE RABBIT HOLE by Norman Spinrad
PACIFIST by Mack Reynolds
YOUR SOLDIER UNTO DEATH by Michael Walker
AND THEN THE DARK--by James Sallis
THE WEAPON by Fredric Brown
OR ELSE by Henry Kuttner
THE LIBERATION OF EARTH by William Tenn
CRAB APPLE CRISIS by George MacBeth
THE HOUSE BY THE CRAB APPLE TREE by S. S.
 Johnson

174 Combat SF. Ed. Gordon R. Dickson. Garden City: Doubleday, 1975. 204pp.

INTRODUCTION by Gordon R. Dickson

THE LAST COMMAND by Keith Laumer
MEN OF GOOD WILL by Ben Bova and Myron R. Lewis
THE PAIR by Joe Hensley
THE BUTCHER'S BILL by David Drake
SINGLE COMBAT by Joe Green
THE MAN WHO CAME EARLY by Poul Anderson

(Combat SF)
   PATRON OF THE ARTS by Fred Saberhagen
   TIME PIECE by Joe W. Haldeman
   RICOCHET ON MIZA by Gordon R. Dickson
   NO WAR, OR BATTLE'S SOUND by Harry Harrison
   HIS TRUTH GOES MARCHING ON by Jerry Pournelle
   THE HORRORS OF WAR by Gene Wolfe

175   Study War No More: A Selection of Alternatives.
      Ed. Joe Haldeman.   New York: St. Martin's
      Press, 1977.   278pp.

      INTRODUCTION by Joe Haldeman

      BASILISK by Harlan Ellison
      THE DUELING MACHINE by Ben Bova
      A MAN TO MY WOUNDING by Poul Anderson
      COMMANDO RAID by Harry Harrison
      CURTAINS by Geo. Alec Effinger
      MERCENARY by Mack Reynolds
      RULE GOLDEN by Damon Knight
      THE STATE OF ULTIMATE PEACE by William Nabors
      BY THE NUMBERS by Isaac Asimov
      TO HOWARD HUGHES: A MODEST PROPOSAL by Joe
         Haldeman

Women

176 The Venus Factor. Ed. Vic Ghidalia and Roger
    Elwood. New York: Manor Books, 1972. 192pp.
    [paper].

    GOD GRANTE THAT SHE LYE STILLE by Cynthia
        Asquith
    THE FOGHORN by Gertrude Atherton
    THE LAST SEANCE by Agatha Christie
    AGAINST AUTHORITY by Miriam Allen deFord
    J-LINE TO NOWHERE by Zenna Henderson
    THE SHIP WHO DISAPPEARED by Anne McCaffrey
    THE LADY WAS A TRAMP by Judith Merrill
    THE DARK LAND by C. L. Moore

177 When Women Rule. Ed. Sam Moskowitz. New York:
    Walker, 1972. 221pp.

    WHEN WOMEN RULE [Introduction] by Sam Moskowitz

    THE AMAZONS by Herodotus
    THE QUEEN OF CALIFORNIA by Garcia Ordonez de
        Montalvo [Translated and with notes by Edward
        Everett Hale]
    THE REVOLT OF THE--- by Robert Barr
    JUNE 6, 2016 by George Allan England
    THE VEILED FEMINISTS OF ATLANTIS by Booth
        Tarkington
    THE LAST MAN by Wallace G. West
    THE LAST WOMAN by Thomas S. Gardner, Ph.D. ˏ
    THE FEMININE METAMORPHOSIS by David H. Keller,
        M.D.
    THE PRIESTESS WHO REBELLED by Nelson S. Bond

178 Women of Wonder: Science Fiction Stories by
Women About Women. Ed. Pamela Sargent. New
York: Vintage Books, 1975. 285pp. [paper].

INTRODUCTION: WOMEN AND SCIENCE FICTION by
Pamela Sargent

THE CHILD DREAMS by Sonya Dorman
THAT ONLY A MOTHER by Judith Merril
CONTAGION by Katherine MacLean
THE WIND PEOPLE by Marion Zimmer Bradley
THE SHIP WHO SANG by Anne McCaffrey
WHEN I WAS MISS DOW by Sonya Dorman
THE FOOD FARM by Kit Reed
BABY, YOU WERE GREAT by Kate Wilhelm
SEX AND/OR MR. MORRISON by Carol Emshwiller
VASTER THAN EMPIRES AND MORE SLOW by Ursula K.
   Le Guin
FALSE DAWN by Chelsea Quinn Yarbro
NOBODY'S HOME by Joanna Russ
OF MIST, AND GRASS, AND SAND by Vonda N.
   McIntyre

179 Aurora: Beyond Equality. Ed. Susan Janice
Anderson and Vonda N. McIntyre. Greenwich, CT:
Fawcett Gold Medal, 1976. 222pp. [paper].

INTRODUCTION: FEMINISM AND SCIENCE FICTION:
BEYOND BEMS AND BOOBS by Susan Janice
Anderson

YOUR FACES, O MY SISTERS! YOUR FACES FILLED OF
   LIGHT! by Raccoona Sheldon
HOUSTON, HOUSTON, DO YOU READ? by James Tiptree,
   Jr.
THE MOTHERS, THE MOTHERS, HOW EERILY IT SOUNDS
   by Dave Skal
THE ANTRIM HILLS by Mildred Downey Broxon
IS GENDER NECESSARY? by Ursula K. Le Guin
CORRUPTION by Joanna Russ
HERE BE DRAGONS by P. J. Plauger

(Aurora)
WHY HAS THE VIRGIN MARY NEVER ENTERED THE WIG-
   WAM OF STANDING BEAR?. by Craig Strete
WOMAN ON THE EDGE OF TIME by Marge Piercy

OTHER WORKS OF INTEREST
ABOUT THE AUTHORS

180   More Women of Wonder: Science Fiction Novelettes
       by Women about Women.   Ed. Pamela Sargent.
       New York: Vintage Books, 1976. 305pp. [paper].

       INTRODUCTION by Pamela Sargent

       JIREL MEETS MAGIC by C. L. Moore
       THE LAKE OF THE GONE FOREVER by Leigh Brackett
       THE SECOND INQUISITION by Joanna Russ
       THE POWER OF TIME by Josephine Saxton
       THE FUNERAL by Kate Wilheim
       TIN SOLDIER by Joan D. Vinge
       THE DAY BEFORE THE REVOLUTION by Ursula K.
          Le Guin

       FURTHER READING
       ABOUT THE AUTHORS
       ABOUT THE EDITOR

181   The New Women of Wonder: Recent Science Fiction
       Stories by Women about Women.   Ed. Pamela Sar-
       gent. New York: Vintage Books, 1978. 363pp.
       [paper].

       INTRODUCTION by Pamela Sargent

       VIEW FROM THE MOON STATION by Sonya Dorman
       SCREWTOP by Vonda N. McIntyre
       THE WARLORD OF SATURN'S MOONS by Eleanor Arnason
       THE TRIUMPHANT HEAD by Josephine Saxton
       THE HEAT DEATH OF THE UNIVERSE by Pamela Zoline
       SONGS OF WAR by Kit Reed
       THE WOMEN MEN DON'T SEE by James Tiptree, Jr.
       DEBUT by Carol Emshwiller

Women

Author Index

This index contains both anthology editors and story authors. The code numbers for anthology editors have been underlined.

149

Title Index

This index contains both anthology and story titles. The code numbers for anthology titles have been underlined.

Title Index

167

Title Index

Title Index

185

Title Index